MW01166029

THE BADGE

Stories and Tales From
Both Sides of the Law

Chuck Klein

BeachHouse Books
Chesterfield Missouri, USA

The Badge --Stories and Tales from Both Sides of the Law

© 2011 Chuck Klein

Cover graphics is a work of Dr. Robert J. Banis. using photos from the author's collection, the badge featured on the front cover was modified from the US government graphic In the public domain http://en.wikipedia.org/wiki/File:BIA_Police_Officer_Badge.jpg#glo balusage.
ISBN 9781596300712

Library of Congress Cataloging-in-Publication Data

Klein, Chuck, 1942-

The badge : stories and tales from both sides of the law / Chuck Klein.

p. cm.

ISBN 978-1-59630-071-2 (alk. paper)

1. True crime stories--United States. 2. Crime--United States--Fiction. 3. Small cities--United States. I. Title.

HV6521.K57 2011

363.2'30973--dc23

2011020391

BeachHouse
Books

www.beachhousebooks.com

BeachHouse Books
An imprint of
  Science & Humanities Press
Chesterfield, Missouri, USA

PREFACE

Although there may be a few changes in details, such as names of the subjects and addresses, all of these stories are based on historically and technically correct personal experiences of my years as a sworn law enforcement officer, licensed private investigator and not-so-law-abiding hot-rodder. Some are verbatim true, some fiction, some a combination and one is an essay.

Having tired of reading monographic style short story books set in big cities, I resolved to write a mixture of small town police and private detective accounts – both fiction and non-fiction. With the exception of the Boomers & Bos story, which was set at the turn of the Century, all other tales occur during the time period of the 1950s to the 1990s.

The Glossary at the back of the book explains some of the terms used in this text.

One final note: Various tactics and procedures used by police and P.I.s, in these stories, though not necessarily illegal today, were in common use then.

Chuck Klein, 2011

For

Allie

Chas

Reily

Adam

Ryann

Sarah

Ryder

Erika

FOREWORD

Reading Chuck Klein's work over the years, I was startled by the imagination on display in this collection—except that I soon realized that it wasn't solely imagination, or even just deft writing, but something equally rare and initially disorienting: an unflinching description of a reality foreign to many of us.

The fact is, most American police departments—despite what Hollywood and the popular press might have you believe—aren't big. The streets in this country many cops patrol are less brightly lighted and less densely packed, and, as Hollywood would therefore have it, less glamorous. Well, glamour be damned. Set mostly in the rural Midwest, Klein tells us of cops and bad guys and ordinary people strung out in extraordinary circumstances, for whom their realities are no less true, no less existential, no less fascinating than those more popularly depicted. He tells it as only a man himself a small-town cop could.

Reflecting the actuality of police work, the stories in this collection run a dizzying gamut. From a protagonist who, stark naked, confronts a psychotic home invader to the officer who offers himself, amid a hail of bullets, to assure the demise of a ready cop-killer to deducing the rollicking night of a drunken medical doctor, these are the stories of a man who's been there with keen and aware eyes to take it in.

In the end, these stories are about people who stand up for the law, but not only the law. These are tales of people acting, often against prevailing odds, in defense of citizens who aren't in positions to defend themselves. Therefore, this collection concerns itself with morality as much as legality. A developed conscience and sense of decency permeates these tales, despite the sometimes unflattering popular image of small-town cops.

"It's easy to keep your cool when you carry a badge and gun," Klein writes about visiting an all-white drinking establishment off duty with a black cop against whom a segment of the crowd suddenly turns. The black cop, in full view of this belligerent bunch, coolly transfers his gun from one pocket to another: silence as the two cops leave. If there's a lesson there for you, it's not a simple one.

Glamour is one thing. What Chuck Klein has written is much more than that and a welcome corrective to the popular depiction of American police work. What's more, it's a hell of a read and a tribute to all those who toil far from the limelight.

Crawford Coates, Managing Editor

ELSEVIER PUBLIC SAFETY

Law Officer magazine

• LawOfficer.com

• LawOfficerConnect.com

Contents

Chapter 1
ALWAYS ASSUME THE WORST

KA-POW, KA-POW, KA-POW the sound of the .357 Magnum reverberated off the walls of the family room . . . I reached for the remote to terminate the inane slaughter of television violence.

Killing the room lights brought instant darkness to compliment the deafening quiet as I stepped out onto the deck. Now the only sound to penetrate the solitude of our secluded haven on the shores of Goose Creek Bay, was that of a Great Horned Owl and the light rustling of leaves from the wisps of a soft summer breeze.

Complacency and tranquility could only describe my feelings as I followed the planking surrounding this picture-windowed cedar home, nestled among the trees of our 144 acre Hoosier farm. Admiring the view of the Kentucky hills across the Ohio River and its smattering of manmade lights, I walked the length of the deck to our bedroom.

After undressing in preparation to shower, I moved back outside to gather some towels that had been left to dry on the rail earlier in the day. Turning to retrace the two steps to the bedroom's sliding-screen door, I was stunned to see the outline of a man, his feet firmly planted, standing halfway down the deck. A quick glance was all I needed to see that this invader of placidity was about my size, had heavy, bushy, dark hair and . . . AND he had something in his hand, AND that something, was pointing at me!

Having been a police officer and a private investigator I've been in tight spots before, but standing naked on my own property, this guy really got my attention! With my eyes riveted on the thing leveled at me while struggling to reach the door, I yelled , "WHO ARE YOU . . . GET OUT OF

HERE." He didn't say anything and as best I could see his expressionless blank stare didn't change.

Stumbling, crashing, running into the house, slamming the screen door closed behind me, I saw out of the corner of my eye, that the trespasser was now advancing toward my end of the deck. The thoughts that went through my mind as I raced to the bureau where I kept a gun, ran from . . ."This must be a friend playing a joke on me and he's going to burst out laughing any second," to . . ."this could only be a sleaze bag from some past arrest or investigation who had sworn to get me."

In what seemed like an inordinate amount of time, I reached the dresser - hang on now - just give me half a second. The muscles in my back tensed in preparation for the bullet that was sure to come as my brain strained to scan all enemies, past and present.

Snatching the pistol from a drawer full of socks, I whirled around, dropped to the floor behind the bed and came up with the classic two-hand hold directed at the screen door whose frame was now filled by the stranger. The silent stranger with something in his hand.

Again I hollered for the man to leave or tell me what he wanted or who he was - anything. No response. He just stood there in the shadows while the harsh incandescence light from the bathroom spotlighted me. Now I could detect that the ominous object in his hand had something sticking out of it - like a barrel!

I waited, listening, looking for the flash of fire that was surely only moments away. Maybe the screen will deflect the bullet, maybe he'll miss, maybe . . . . The years of police indoctrination took hold as I resigned myself to empty my gun into this intruder before I died. I strained to see, almost hoping to discern a flash of fire that would bring this confrontation to a very climatic and final end. My death threat didn't move, didn't make a sound. The screen rippled. It might have been the wind. The hair on the back of my neck stood up.

I had to think, go over my options, form a plan, I couldn't take my eyes off the thing in his hand. Surely this isn't real - too much TV!

I didn't have to shoot unless he shot first or unless I was sure it was a weapon he was holding and he gave some indication that he was going to use it. Since I was home alone I could even allow him to enter the house, and as long as he didn't try to get too close or actually assault me, I could just play this thing out. I really wanted to know who he was . . . and, why?

The bed afforded enough cover that I didn't want to risk trying for the phone to call the sheriff or a neighbor - the nearest being over a half mile to the west. Besides the police would be at least 20 minutes away since there was only one on-duty officer for the entire county. I could make a dash for the hallway where I could hide, but if he shot me as I ran I wouldn't be able to return the favor. Besides he could hide too and wait until I went to bed or my wife and sons came home and then attack.

Half lying, half sitting, still undressed, light shining on me and my legs beginning to cramp I continued to shout, "WHO ARE YOU... WHAT DO YOU WANT...GET OUT OF HERE OR I'LL BLOW YOU AWAY, MAN!"

My imagination was running wild. Maybe he was just guarding the door so the real perp could slip in the front and sneak up behind me. I tried to be cognizant of my peripheral vision, lest I take my eyes from what has to be some form of lethal and instant destruction hidden by the screen. I held my breath so not even the sound of my breathing could mask another invader.

3

Then, still without so much as a word, he turned and started back down the deck. In a flash I killed the light in the bathroom and pulled on a pair of shorts then ran toward the hall. I don't know why I took the time to put on my briefs, but it made me feel better, less vulnerable.

Reaching the entrance way, I saw through the kitchen window, that he had reached the end of the deck. He froze as I covered him with light from the driveway floods while opening the door and taking careful aim. He was less than twenty feet from me now and I could see what was in his hand. It was a pencil and pad of paper.

He could have been killed. I might have shot him. My head felt hot and at the same time a chill came over my whole body. I'd had men in my sights before, but this was different. I was just doing my job then, this was personal - this was home to my wife and children!

I motioned for him to come over where he displayed a message on the pad reading, "My Father says I'm a very special person". The stranger was a mentally handicapped, deaf mute!

Keeping my distance I put the gun down and took his pad. After writing notes back and forth he finally told me who he was. He seemed shy, so I invited him in the kitchen for a Coke while I telephoned his family who promised to send someone right up. I learned from further note writing that he had often admired our house from the road and just wanted to see it up close. He had driven his car only part way up the quarter mile driveway, with his lights out, and had walked the rest of the way.

End of story? Not quite. The next day I learned that he was a walk-away from a state mental hospital, committed by his family because he was prone to violence and had attacked people during previous encounters. On this occasion he had savagely beaten his aged father before stealing the car he used to visit me. His brother told me the family wouldn't have held it against me if I had killed him.

I was relieved that the taking of a human life hadn't been necessary, but I was also comforted that I had subscribed to the old country adage: "The door might not always be locked, but the gun is always loaded". Maybe he had wanted more than just a look, but the gun scared him. What if the gun hadn't been available or what if the kids or my wife had been home and one of them had been the first to encounter him, what if . . . .

Chapter 2
FIRST TIME BEHIND THE BADGE

"Chief? What can I do to help? I'm available day or night."

"Do you own a handgun?"

"Yes sir."

"Wear it, along with dark pants and a blue shirt and be in my office seven o'clock tonight." Cool!

Wow! This is going to be way cool. Here I was a junior executive with our family paper-converting business and not too many years from my last encounter as a hot-rodding chasee. Now, I was about to become the chaser. Living in Amberley Village, a small bedroom community contiguous to Cincinnati, I had phoned the police chief to volunteer my time.

It was 1968 and cities all across the country were under siege from riots, looting and burning. No one knew what direction the rioters would take – stick to destruction of their own neighborhoods or branch out to the mostly white suburbs. All white Amberley, under a county wide mutual-aid agreement, had already sent two of their officers to augment the city where the crux of the rioting had been taking place.

Before leaving my comfortable and secure home, I made my wife strap on a holster and gun, telling her not to open the door to anyone. And if someone breaks in – shoot him. Don't talk to him. Don't warn him. Just empty the gun into him. Then try (lines might be jammed) to call the police.

Arriving at the station, in my black wool trousers, blue button-down, oxford cloth shirt and a snub-nose .38 in a hip holster, I was shown to the Chief's office. With a glance up to me, Chief Krueger reached into his desk, produced a badge, and with the command to 'pin it on,' said, "You're now a deputy police officer. Tell the rest of the men to assemble in the squad room." Heavy!

My introduction to the Amberley Village Police Department – as an adult - began in the early 1960s (age 20) through Patrolman Tony Bloomberg. He was a square shooter and we seemed to get along well. I used to visit him when he worked dispatch on the 3rd shift. One subject of discussion was how many times I saw one of his fellow officers, while on duty, hanging out at Frisch's, an out-of-village restaurant. Not only did he kill time at Frisch's, but he would respond to fight calls at Castle Farm and other non Amberley details - sometimes code-3.

Tony asked me to keep a written list of the dates and times I witnessed this officer in an APD scout car in non-village locations. After a month or so, I turned my list over to Bloomberg. I think it might have helped him get sergeant stripes and maybe also could have been instrumental in the dismissal of this slacker officer.

With all police officers crowded in the office, the Chief told what he had learned from earlier meetings with other area police chiefs. Rumors of mass black invasions of white communities were rampant, but no one was sure which way things might go. Krueger sent us out to patrol the five-square mile village with these words: "I don't want any of my men hurt - if any of those rioters (might have used different word) so much as touches anyone of you - kill him." Heavy, my kitty! I rode with a sergeant until about midnight and again the next night. This was fun and somewhere in the back of my mind a light began to glow.

With my life-long interest in guns/shooting, I worked on a novel concept, instinct shooting with a handgun. These experiments coupled with a new found ability to write

7

resulted in my first paid article in Law & Order Magazine (this brainchild later led to a book on the subject – see Glossary: Instinct Combat Shooting). Krueger encouraged me to pursue a career in LE and helped by sending me to one of the first NRA Police Firearms Instructor courses and by writing a letter of recommendation. The Chief indicated he would hire me if I moved out of Amberley, but I wanted more action than a nice quiet bedroom community. Krueger also gave me a significant hint as to what police work is all about. He reiterated what one of his officers told him that cemented his hiring. This, then candidate, told the chief he liked being in a position of being able to help people. I realized I felt the same way and is the reason I became a police officer and later a volunteer fire fighter and a member of Kiwanis International.

Though the family business was busy and I was making good money, I was disillusioned with the direction of certain aspects of our country. I didn't see myself as a placard carrying protester – and being cannon fodder in Nam was also not an option. Police work seemed like a way I could make my contribution to society. In 1971, I found full time employment with the Village of Woodlawn, Ohio Police Department.

Everyone should have at least one job in his or her lifetime where they start each day with the revelation, "You mean they pay me to do this"?

Applying to police agencies, my biggest worry was my juvenile record. During the late 1950s, and between the ages of 15 and 18, I had been involved in a number of . . . ah, not too bright activities – such as moving traffic violations and "disagreements" with my father. Some of these activities resulted in trips to Juvenile Detention. On one such occasion, I was handcuffed and hauled to the

Amberley station where, after cooling my heels for a short while, then Captain Krueger, without saying a word, approached me, removed the cuffs, walked to the door, opened it, removed his service revolver, snapped it open to make sure it was loaded and finally said, "We don't have to take you to Juvenile. Go ahead; you can walk out that door. But you better run fast, because I'm going to shoot you in the back if you do." This was big time and I was just a punk. I looked at my shoes. The Captain then said to the Sergeant, "Take him to Juvenile and if he tries to run, shoot him." Heavy, my kitty!

A night in the "cooler" and my heels were frigid. I was beaten and ready to kowtow to authority – at least until I got my bravado back. In court the next day, and with my parents present, I apologized for my recent behavior and promised to be a good boy. The Judge, Benjamin Schwartz, in no uncertain words told me he never wanted to see me in his court room again.

> *As fate would have it, and on another day, there I stood in the same court room. After the proceedings were over it was obvious the Judge had forgotten his threat. I approached the bench, hat in hand, and said, "Excuse me your Honor, but the last time I was here you told me you never wanted to see me in your court room again." Judge Schwartz broke out into a huge grin, climbed down from behind the bench and shook my hand. It was 13 years later and I was the arresting officer of a young juvenile offender.*

This kind of "anti-social" behavior might have deterred others from pursuing a career in law enforcement. However, for me, I was lucky to have Bill Krueger as my captain/chief. He was the type of man who could look beyond juvenile pranks and difficult father/son relations to see the good in individuals. He also had a unique perspective about life experiences. On a later visit to his office, he told me of a candidate for one the department's openings who had an exemplary high school record. Not only did this young police officer hopeful excel in class, but he had never been in a fistfight or had even been sent to the principal's office for any sort of transgression or trouble. The Chief didn't hire him citing the reason that such a person might not be able to deal with, and empathize with persons he would have to confront as a police officer. I sure had an over abundance of negative experiences, but I had never committed a felony and I had shown remorse when hauled before the authorities.

Felony convictions can haunt for a lifetime – ask any inmate.

Woodlawn was exciting work resulting in the opportunities to make felony arrests for crimes ranging from gun dealing to rape to armed robbery to murder. But one of the most horrific events I witnessed, ironically, occurred in Amberley. I was on my way home after working the 2nd as the Amberley fire trucks rolled onto Ridge Road. Still being in uniform, I followed, thinking, they might need me to help with traffic. It was a house fire in the new part of Elbrook. As the men fought the fire, I made a coffee run to Frisch's. Officer Currens was injured when he used his bare hands to break the window where the children slept – all three died. Though it was traumatizing to know children were in that house, there is no word for what I later learned.

A day or two after the fire, I visited APD. Krueger played the interview tapes of the home owner (I knew him personally) and his wife. He explained how he tried to fight the fire and told his wife to call the fire department after getting the children out. She talked about how she chased their dogs trying to save them and then said, "All is not lost,

I still have my dogs." It was difficult to conceive how she cherished her dogs more than her children. The fire department was called by a neighbor - well after the home was enflamed.

Meanwhile, in less than six months on the job at Woodlawn, I was told by Sgt. Paul Roddic that he, the WPD chief and others were part of a theft ring and if I didn't play along they would shoot me in the knees. This all happened while I was working my first 3rd with Roddic. During these late night shifts I witnessed him using his collection of keys to local businesses to steal things. Knowing I couldn't go to my chief, I visited Krueger - a man I knew I could trust. He made notes of our conversation and set up a meeting with the FBI. They told me to keep a record of the sergeant's transgressions and report back weekly. After the criminal officer's girl friend turned him in, my reports were part of the evidence used to help convince him to plead guilty. Former Sergeant Roddic went to prison. The WPD chief knew that I knew he was involved and it caused him to continue my probation and finally to recommend not hiring me.

I was broken-hearted, but felt I needed to clear my name and thus applied to other police agencies. The Village of Terrace Park, Ohio had an opening and Chief Hiett told me if I can pass a polygraph test, the job was mine. I passed as I had done nothing wrong at Woodlawn. Though my reputation was clear, I wasn't making enough money to live on and I resigned before completing a full year.

By the late 70s Amberley was no longer the neighbor-friendly, country village I grew up in and thus began a search for an old-time, small community to raise my family. I found Switzerland County, Indiana. Here, my sons enjoyed shooting, hunting, riding motorcycles and I

11

began new careers as a Private Detective and writer. I also spent seven years in the 80s as one of Sheriff J. D. Leap's reserve officers and ten years as a state trained volunteer firefighter for Patriot.

Everyone should put something back into his or her community.

Chapter 3
FLASHING BLUE LIGHTS

The first shot tore through his upper leg exiting just below the hip. The second and third shot hit . . . .

~~~~~~~~~~~~

He lay on the extra firm, queen sized mattress under a sheet and light wool blanket listening to the sounds of the city. The bike ride had helped but he still felt itchy. It was almost midnight, and all he had done for the last hour was stare at the dancing lights on the ceiling. Somewhere close by emergency vehicles' sirens wailed and yelped. They passed his apartment causing the beacons – the blue flashing beacons – to play tag with the other lights that bounced off his ceiling, walls and mirrors. The tough ex-cop/private detective/motorcycle rider closed his eyes and fought the twenty some-odd-year old nightmare . . . .

~~~~~~~~~~~~

Keying the mic and activating the roof lights all with one movement, Sergeant Travis Tarvon calmly gave his car number, "Four-John- Eleven."

"4-John -11," the dispatcher echoed.

"Possible DUI, farm-to-market, four-three-two, four miles west of eight-twenty-one. Older model Ford sedan, blue in color, bears Texas Tom-Adam-Sam-nine-nine-eight."

"Eight-William-Eight. Car 8-William-8."

"8-William-8."

"8-William-8 are you clear on 4-John-11's location? Possible DUI?"

"Affirmative. I'm south bound eight-twenty. Be about fifteen."

A jack rabbit, highlighted by the headlights of both vehicles, scampered across the highway as the patrol car's spotlight lit up the interior of the losermobile. The blue flashing lights were swallowed in the pitch black of the West Texas prairie. In the grimy Ford he could see three subjects, two males and a female. The driver slowed and put two wheels on the gravel shoulder kicking up a cloud of dust. Nobody was making any frantic moves like they were trying to hide contraband or weapons. It looked like a routine stop.

Just before exiting his car the radio broke squelch, "4-John-11, no wants NCIC, Texas Tom-Adam-Sam-nine-nine-eight."

"4-John-11 okay. 2-7."

"2-7, 4-John-11. Oh-one-forty-four hours. KQA-two-three-oh."

At the open window, the experienced officer noted the distinct odor of alcoholic beverage on the driver's breath and a half empty whiskey bottle on the back seat. The occupants, dirty, scruffy and smelly, all appeared to be in their thirties. The female, in a tube top and seated in the shotgun seat, seemed to be spaced out. The small framed back seat passenger watched with intense but dilated eyes.

"I'm stopping you, sir, because you drove off the road in two places back there. May I see your operator's license, please," Travis commanded in a firm but polite tone.

The man with a two day's growth of beard said his name was Tom Hickey. After a few minutes of fumbling in his wallet and scattering the contents of the glove box all over the front seat, he claimed he couldn't find his license or registration. "You're going to have to step out of the car,

14

sir," Travis said, opening the driver's door while trying to watch everybody's hands at once.

He led the man, who was about his size, to the rear of the cruiser and well out of view of the passengers. Travis ran the driver through a series of divided-skills evaluations and horizontal gaze nystagmus for documentation purposes in case of a contested court hearing. The Sergeant had an uneasy feeling. This man was more than just drunk. He could have stalled until his back-up arrived, but he felt if he could just put the cuffs on him, he and the others would be easier to control. "I'm going to have to arrest you for driving under the influence."

"Aw, c'mon man. I can handle it. You've seen worse. C'mon let me go," Hickey whined.

With a sigh of capitulation, the arrestee turned to place his hands on the trunk of the cruiser as the deputy tucked his flashlight under his arm. Then sort of as an afterthought the rotted tooth, whiskey breathed bully turned back. "Aw man, officer," he said looking at Travis's name tag. "Sergeant Tarvon, how 'bout . . . ."

Before he even finished the sentence, sans any warning, and before Travis could react, the brawny man was on him. The flashlight fell as he raised his hands to ward off the attack. The assault was so sudden and from such close proximity he didn't have time to move out of the way. Juiced up on drugs and booze some men can act faster than a cat in heat.

Squeezed into a bear hug Travis knew instantly he was in trouble. Rocking, twisting, kicking, they fell into the ditch next to the roadway, with Travis on the bottom. He immediately felt sharp pain in his rib cage area. They rolled long-ways in the culvert, but Travis was quickly able to pin the man with his left arm while he reached for his portable radio, hoping it would reach from this remote and desolate location.

"FOUR-JOHN-ELEVEN!   TEN-SEVENTY-EIGHTY! FOUR-JOHN-ELEVEN," he barked loudly into the mike, trying not to sound panicky.

The dispatcher, in an even and professional voice immediately responded, "4-John-11 . . . 8-William-8."

"8-William-8, enroute"

"Okay 8-William-8. 4-John-11."

When he received no response, the seasoned dispatcher continued a monotone monologue with run-together words and sentences that only cops can decipher. "Attention all cars all departments unit 4-John-11 requesting a 10-78 last twenty is farm-to-market four-three-two four miles west of state route eight-twenty-one involves Ford sedan blue in color bearing Texas Tom-Adam-Sam-nine-nine-eight 4-John-11."

Travis heard only the heavy breathing and grunts of the man named Hickey.

All across the county every officer with a radio, on-duty or off, began speeding toward the dreaded officer-needs-assistance call. None acknowledged the call or asked permission, fearing that their transmission might override additional information from 4-John-11. One patrolman, in the middle of writing a ticket, suddenly and without a word let the astonished motorist go before racing, code three, to help his brother officer.

Hickey retorted with what could only be described as super human strength. Travis, all two hundred and ten pounds of him, was suddenly thrown across the ditch. Dazed and still trying to get his feet under him, he saw in the strobe light syncopation of the blue flashing emergency lights the foul smelling brute pouncing and screaming, "I'M GOING TO KILL YOU, YOU DIRTY BASTARD!"

~~~~~~~~~~~~~~~

Travis had begun to perspire. He hadn't faced his demon in a long time. Maybe he could put it behind him if he looked at it in an objective way. Fat chance. The emotions were and probably would always be too strong. He should have; no, no he wasn't going to play the shoulda, woulda, coulda game tonight. It was pointless. Tonight he would be human, a fallible human being who is not perfect. Tonight he would try to forgive himself. Because if he didn't, how could he expect anyone else to.

~~~~~~~~~~~~~~~

As the assailant pounded with his fists, Travis hammered his face with the radio until it shattered. The two men fought for survival in a blackened, muddy ditch lit only by the intermittent flashes of the blue lights. They rolled in the damp mud as Hickey clamped a headlock on the officer with one arm while his free hand ripped Travis's hair. Travis broke the hold when he grabbed Hickey's crotch, squeezing with all his might while biting the heathen's forearm. The taste of blood and sweat fed his animal instincts, intensifying his need to survive.

Suddenly free of each other, Hickey struggled to get up, spewing death threats, while Travis scratched at his holster. To Travis the surrealism of the pseudo time deception phenomenon, tachyinterval, only made the onset of panic more pronounced. He was amazed at how much information his mind could process at a time like this. "Why was it taking so long for his gun to come into battery? Why was his arm taking so long to block the foot that was coming at his head? Where was his back-up? Did the 10-78 call get out? Where were the other occupants of the car?"

The kick, only partially blocked, knocked his service revolver out of his hand and somewhere behind him. The force of Hickey's full leg kick temporarily caused the man to lose his momentum – time for Travis to scramble for the gun. Frantically probing the weeds and debris, he found the weapon and rolled on his side at the instant Hickey leapt on him raining blows to his face. He knew he had to shoot this crazed superman before he lost consciousness but this scumbag, like he read Travis's mind, grabbed the three-fifty-seven with both hands and turned it toward the Sergeant's face. The two adversaries, now literally nose to nose fought for control. Travis, aware that his finger was exerting pressure on the trigger, maneuvered his left hand to clamp the cylinder and prevent it from being fired. Hickey twisted the magnum into Travis's chest and, still eyeball to eyeball spat, "I'm gonna kill you!" Summoning all his dwindling strength, Travis forced his knees up and with a mighty thrust catapulted gun and man over his head.

Exhausted, arms trembling, Travis clawed at his pants leg and the .38 snub-nose back-up gun strapped to an ankle holster. Eyes riveted on Hickey, highlighted by the eerie glow of the cruiser's taillights, he watched in horror as the big brute leveled the magnum at him. Struggling to bring the small stainless steel revolver into battery Travis heard himself screaming, "NO! NO! NO!"

At less than six feet apart and almost simultaneously, the two weapons spit fire at each other blinding the shooters in brilliant flashes of white hot death. Hickey's first shot tore through Travis's upper leg exiting just below the hip. His second and third shot hit the dirt to the left of the deputy's head. Travis, eyes locked on a shirt chest button, emptied his five shot Chief's Special. Hickey stood stock still.

Completely baffled, Travis thought, "I couldn't have missed him!" The wide-eyed man, the one with the three-fifty-seven, then jumped out of the ditch and ran across the road and into the darkness.

Injured, exhausted and with an empty gun Travis fought to control the onset of panic. Fishing for his pocket knife – his last line of defense – he searched the roadside fearing he'd catch a glimpse of Hickey returning.

Now large numbers of blue flashing lights uniformly lit the area as the back-ups started to arrive. When you're down, out and in need of help nothing, absolutely nothing, is more comforting, even to a cop, than the presence of a fresh, clean and bright-eyed uniformed officer. Fellow knights in blue with brightly colored arm patches, shiny badges and lots of guns covered the scene. These calm and organized keepers of the peace applied first-aid to Travis, took care of securing the other occupants of the sedan and ordered the ambulance. With flashlights and riot guns at the ready they fanned out and searched for Hickey.

Of Travis's five shots, four struck the intended target. Two of the one-hundred-twenty-five grain semi-jacketed hollow points had ripped the man's heart apart. His body, pumped up on adrenaline and high on alcohol and drugs, had powered him for over a hundred feet into the prairie. He never even knew he was dead.

～～～～～～～～～～～～～

Travis was drenched in perspiration, his heart beat hard and fast. The dancing lights on his ceiling were gone. He touched the scars on his leg to reassure himself that they were in fact long healed. In the bathroom he rinsed his mouth with Scope to take away the taste of blood and sweat.

He hadn't gone through the whole scenario in a long time – it seemed easier like maybe his mind was also healing. The face that grimaced back at him from the mirror told him that the guilt that had been eating at him all these years was gone. Tonight for the first time he faced the fact that, although he had killed a man, his action was excusable and justifiable. Tonight he could forgive himself and tonight, for the first time, he was certain that God had forgiven him.

Chapter 4
THE P. I.

The piercing light was visible long before he heard the two longs followed by two shorts as the Chicago bound James Whitcome Riley approached the Carter Street crossing. Within minutes the E-9, the most powerful of diesel engines, was thundering into Winton Place station. Though the little two piece windshield, just aft of the giant single head lamp, towered over his head he couldn't suppress the smile and memory of last week's Christmas. Then it was he who towered over an E-9, a Lionel with "Santa Fe" splashed in orange and silver across the side of his gift to a wide-eyed nephew.

From his vantage point, near the Western Union window, Kurt Kidwell could see the platform to the right and the parking lot to his left. The target was nowhere to be found. Maybe Miss Dolly had set him up - they were traveling by car and it was a bum steer. He watched, ticket in hand, as the porters loaded and unloaded boxes, grips, trunks and all sizes of suitcases. He watched the passengers embark and disembark, especially the smart looking tan-suited knockout with the matching hat perched atop her stacked honey blond hair. Kidwell never took his eye off the lot. Maybe he was already on-board having caught the train at the Oakley Station.

The man who earned a living watching, watched, with a sinking feeling, as the Brakeman, lantern in hand, got into position at the rear of the train. It had begun to rain. Kidwell stepped toward the Pullman car, Starlight, as the sound of tires straining for adhesion on gravel commanded his attention. Caught in the head lamps of the a dirty black '49 Cadillac convertible, the trademark of Mr. Pogue, Kidwell pulled the brim of his fedora a little lower and the collar of his trench coat up as he stepped onto the Starlight's platform.

The Brakeman began to move his lantern up and down, the signal for the engineer to get underway. Mr. Pogue and his driver, laden with two suitcases and a string tied cardboard box, had to be helped by the Brakeman onto the now moving train.

He'd give Pogue an hour or so then he'd look him up. He wasn't going anywhere for at least a few hours - the Riley's first stop. Right now Kidwell needed the men's room and some warm food. Entering the day-coach, El Capitan, he searched the overhead racks for a place to stash his hat and coat. Amid leather suitcases, paperboard composite grips and round lady's' hat boxes with the name of swank department stores emblazoned on the richly colored Chrome-Kote wrapping, he found an unobtrusive spot. The car's seats were filled more with small trunks, a few leather trimmed canvas covered grips and gift boxes than the holiday travelers themselves. Tossed on and between were an array of coats and outer wear, a leather flyer's jacket, a smartly creased gentleman's felt hat with a tweed sport jacket and a hangered sailor's dress blues. The lavatory was clean, properly stocked and a great relief.

The dining car was about half full so Kidwell had no trouble settling into a starched linen covered table, complimented with a small bouquet of fresh flowers snugged against the window. Within a minute the hospital-white clad waiter filled Kidwell's order for a Jack Daniels on the rocks. Complacency settled over the Private Investigator as he casually observed soothed couples' happy faces reflected by the individual table lamps against their personal half-shaded windows. They dined on choice Prime Rib, Boursin Chicken or Stuffed Lemon Sole as America's backyards roll by. The dressed to the nines, tan-suited knockout smiled at him over the top of a tall cold exotic something. Kurt Kidwell discretely adjusted his shoulder holster before approaching tan-suit.

"I'm Karl Kinder, may I join you?" he asked, athletically jostling his muscular body into the opposite seat as the train rocked over a set of switches. The pseudo name was one he used when dealing with strangers while on the job. In this business, you never know who's also on the job on the opposite side.

"Seems that you already have, and I'm happy to meet you, I think. My name is Victoria and that, that drunken soldier who just came in has been bothering me. Uh, oh, here he comes again."

"Well . . . there you are little lady. I thought I lost ya. Is thesh man bothering you," the three-stripe non-com slurred.

"I think it's the other way around, Sergeant. The lady is with me so please refrain from interfering with us again," Kurt said, in a kind manner, rising from his seat while boring his eyes into a set of slightly dilated pupils.

It was really all one move, the words, the stare and the arm lock that crumpled the uniform to his knees. Reducing the pressure enough to allow the intruder to be half dragged, Kidwell deposited the rude soldier in the forward sleeper admonishing him to sleep it off.

Returning to his upholstered dinner table chair beneath the car length, hand-painted murals covering the frieze on both sides of the older 1937 era dining car, the lady named Victoria smiled again, "Thank you ever so much, Mr. Kinder." The soft pastel colors highlighted by the hanging globe lights lent an aura of mystic and intrigue to this calm and sophisticated lady.

During the interlude that preceded the main course the widowed heir to an old manufacturing company and the gentleman with the clandestine demeanor, discretely exchanged pleasantries.

They dined on filet mignon with sautéed mushrooms and fresh spinach au gratin. When the plates had been cleared they sipped Three Star Hennessey as winking roadside crossings lights occasionally flashed across the darkened window. He told her his business was corporate acquisitions and he, also, was on his way home to Chicago.

The train, now at cruising speeds of seventy plus, set up a gentle rocking motion which, between cars as he was seeing her to her bedroom compartment, caused her to fall into him. He steadied her, feeling firm upper arms and catching a scent of Chanel Number Five. They stood close to let another passenger pass. The vibes oozed. "I've got some business to take care of," he said, locking into her light green eyes. "If I stop back in an hour or so can we have a night cap?"

She returned his gaze before twisting, brushing against his arm, as she unlocked the door, "I'd like that. I need to freshen up a little, anyway."

Since Pogue hadn't visited the dining car he had to be between there and the club car. Kidwell set out to scout the train. The top half of the outside door to the car just ahead of the lounge car was open, a fact noted by the PI in case anything had to be tossed out. Stepping into the club car, the classic model with a half length mahogany bar down one side, Kidwell smiled to the lone bartender as his eyes scanned the room. Seated in the fore section was a businessman studying a newspaper next to his young, comic book reading son and a fidgeting, beer drinking sailor. Halfway back, Mr. Pogue, holding the twine tied box, and his chauffeur were complacently sipping drinks. Kidwell walked the length of the room and sat at the rear most table, after surreptitiously verifying the door to the observation platform was unlocked. The bartender looked up but the private dick shook his head while picking up a Life magazine.

He didn't like the situation. He didn't like all the witnesses. He didn't like the driver, if that's what he really was. If he was a driver, then why did he leave the Caddy at the train station and why did he keep looking around - like a body guard.

The diesel horn sounded, two longs followed by two shorts for the approach of a public crossing. The now tense six foot P.I. had been counting since the first. The engineer had been very punctual. Almost exactly eleven seconds after the first blast of the horn the sound of the crossing bells reached the train's passenger cars. The bells, combined with the flashing red lights bouncing through the train's windows, were quite distracting.

The sailor got up to leave, the P.I. started another magazine. It didn't look like Pogue was in any hurry by the number of olive pits in the ash tray. Body guard was sipping something dark with ice through a straw - probably a Coke if he was on the job. Kidwell had hoped to have concluded the business by now, but there had been too many people and he hadn't counted on a body guard.

The mission had seemed simple enough when the phone call came, followed by the packet of cash and directives. All he had to do was trade the package Mr. Pogue was to be transporting for the cash Kurt was carrying in his inside jacket pocket. He was instructed to secure the package at all costs, something about a threat to national security. It seemed his clientele only called when the task was too tough or sticky for lesser agents.

When the executive and his son rose to leave, Kurt signaled the bartender. He asked the practiced elderly Negro if he would be so kind as to check with the kitchen

25

for an order of cheese and crackers. Now there were only three.

"Mr. Pogue, I'd like a word . . . ."

"Mr. Pogue don't talk to nobody, so take a powder, pal," the burly body guard belched forcing his way between them.

Time was short before the barkeep or another passenger would walk in. Kidwell lowered his eyes and turned slightly to send body language messages of capitulation while he searched for words to stall for time and a piece of luck. Softly he began, "I'm sorry sir, I didn't mean to intrude it's only that . . . the words were lost to the wail of the E-9's horn . . . won't bother . . . eight - nine - ten - the bells clanged, the lights flashed, the bruiser's concentration broke as he glanced out the windows. Just like the sergeant, and so many others before him, it was all one move. The P.I.'s foot found the male tender spot just below the belly button an instant before the right hand connected with the jaw of the stunned and buckling galoot.

Mr. Pogue, impaired by the martinis, could only stare, slack jawed, as Kurt dragged the unconscious body through the rear doors and onto the observation platform. The thought of tossing the dead weight over was tempting, but he had confidence that his body guarding days were over for the night.

"Now then Mr. Pogue, before we were so rudely interrupted, we have business to transact. I have here," Kidwell began extracting the envelope filled with cash from his jacket pocket, "A large sum of money that I intend to trade you for the box on your lap."

"What have you done with Bruno. It's not for sale, now please leave me or I shall summon the authorities. Bartender, bartender . . . ."

26

"I sent him away. It's just you and me. Time is short and you only have two choices."

"What do you mean? Who are you? I'm not selling. All you and your kind want to do is keep it off the market. My invention will . . . ."

As the inventor rambled on, Kidwell took the man's half drained highball from the table top and casually tossed it into his face. The slightly intoxicated keeper of the box reacted before he realized he had relaxed his grip on the box. That was all the practiced P.I. needed. He flipped the envelope on the table and strode out, catching out of the corner of his eye, the opening platform door and the guard struggling in, revolver in hand!

"Is it a present for me?" the golden haired lady impishly chided as she opened the door at his knock. "Or is it a reward from rescuing other maidens?"

His face relaxed and a smile spread to his dimples as he surveyed the room and the silk robe clad lady. But his mind was racing. "Sorry to put you to any trouble, but I'm in a bit of a jam and I might need your help."

He put the box down on the day couch, turned to look her in the eye to see if she was with him. She held her head high and stared back at him. He took her squared shoulders in his powerful hands pulling her toward him. It was a closed mouth kiss, he afraid of relaxing, and she, just to let him know the quid pro quo was sealed.

He told her the box contained medical experiments that a Russian agent, an armed Russian agent on board the train, was trying to steal from him. "Look, I think the train is going to stop soon and when it does I'll need you to get off with me. They won't be looking for a couple, especially one with glasses," he said producing a pair of eye glasses with clear lenses.

It didn't take long before the sound of the thug could be heard in the passage way, banging on every door. There wasn't time to discuss anything.

Bang, bang, bang, "Open the door."

Slowly she opened the door a crack. The bully, gun in hand, pushed, slamming it against the closet. "What's the meaning of this . . . ."

"Shut up. Where is he?"

"How dare you. There's no one in here. Who . . . ." He pushed passed her, looking first toward the beds then at the toilet room door.

Kidwell, crouched, back to the wall, in the tiny, crowded, pitch-black water closet eased his HSc Mauser out of its shoulder holster and leveled it at the door. Over the click-clack of the train's wheels he heard the distinct click of the door handle as the Mauser's safety clicked off.

Having killed before and in control of the situation, fear was absent, though he was, maybe a mite apprehensive. The little 7.65 pocket pistol, taken from a Nazi officer he had garroted during his days in the service of his country, was a favorite of his arsenal of concealable weapons. Its reliability had been established in past operations.

BlaaaaaaaaaaaaCrack,Crack,Crackaaaaaaaat. The timing of the diesel locomotion's announcement that it was approaching a station couldn't have been more opportune.

The aggressor, dumbfounded at the three thirty-two caliber crimson holes in his shirt front, paradoxically glimpsed the lavatory mirror for his final vision - the face of a dead man.

"Victoria, Victoria give me a hand, he's fallen on me."

The previously formal and composed lady Victoria, ashen and wide eyed, nonetheless dutifully straddled the body and extended a hand.

"Get dressed and put on some lipstick, we're getting off here." She stood there, gaping at the corpse as the impact of the situation began to sink in. Struggling with her suit case, he slapped her hard on the rump. "Get moving, NOW!"

With the smaller of her two suitcases he dumped their contents on the bed, placed the string tied box inside, and packed what he could of the dumped contents around the box.

"What we can't get into your other suitcase, I'll replace," he stated, throwing undergarments and personal items into the larger grip as the train slowed for the station stop.

Victoria, displaying genuine aristocratic style, smiled as she accompanied the P.I. through the El Capitan where he retrieved his hat and coat. As a cold wind whipped at their ankles they snuck across the platform to a waiting cab.

The hotel in this out-of-the-way little burg was, if nothing else, a safe haven. Here, as the lady bathed, he inspected the contents of the box he had killed for.

After his shower, and standing in his under shorts, he moved to take her into his arms, "I just want to hold you."

"You mean gratuitously? For helping you conduct whatever dirty business you're in? Perhaps you better tell who you really are, Mr. Karl Kinder, if that's your real name." She had regained her full stature as a business executive. "You have presented yourself as a gentleman, at least in your dealings with me. Please continue to do so. I have no intention of allowing this room to become a tryst."

"I understand and respect your wishes. All I said was I wanted to hold you. I need a little tenderness now and I thought you might also."

"Who are you? What . . . ."

"It's best that you don't know my real name. I'm a private investigator and sometimes my assignments get a little ah . . . hairy. I'm sorry to have involved you in this, but making use of you as cover seemed like a good idea at the time. After this matter is concluded I'd like to try to start all over - on a social level, especially since we're both from Chicago. Right now, I think we both could use a little, make that a lot, of TLC."

She came to him. They hugged. The tension dissipated. In a short while they fell asleep.

Hours later he slipped out, paid the hotel bill and, box in hand, wolfed down a pancake breakfast at a greasy spoon two blocks down the street. Finding himself in the seedier part of town he quickly located a pawn shop where he purchased a used canvas suitcase in which to carry the box.

He caught a cab to the station, bought a ticket on the next train to Chicago and found a public telephone. Three rings and he heard his client, "Consolidated Gas and Oil, Incorporated, may I help you?" the sweet voice of a young operator answered.

"Extension 447, Please"

"Yes."

"This is Kidwell."

"Have you got it?"

"Yes sir."

"Where are you? Tell me what's in the box."

"I'm a couple of hours out of the LaSalle Street Station. The box contains a lot of diagrams, blue prints and legal papers plus what looks like a carburetor - a special kind of carburetor."

"Excellent. Come directly to the Drake. We will meet you in the lobby."

He had a half hour to kill before departure. Maybe he could find a little something for Miss Dolly. She had really come through for him, but the thought of a special lady is what was really twisting around in his mind. He took a walk around the block, past a Negro bar where he stopped to listen to a solo cornetist crying some blues number that drifted by like a spirit on the winds of time.

Author's note: Rumors have circulated for over half a century that a man named Pogue (or Fish or ???) invented a carburetor that produced unprecedented fuel economy. The rumor includes the scenarios that the petroleum producers, foreign interests and/or the automobile manufacturers, to keep the product off the market, stole the design and to keep Mr. Pogue/Fish/??? quiet, paid him off or. . . .

Chapter 5
EVERYDAY HERO

"Four-six-eight. Car 4-6-8, person injured, Woodlawn Food Market, Marion and Wayne. 4-6-8."

"Four-six-eight, okay," I responded to the dispatcher's detail. The time was late afternoon in our small southwestern Ohio village. It had been a quiet Saturday afternoon - one of those lazy spring days when cops do more waving and smiling than anything else. I turned my cruiser around, swung into traffic, and headed toward the food market.

Almost simultaneously my partner, 4-6-9, and I arrived to face a group of bystanders, some with coats, others in jackets and still others in shirt sleeves. It was that kind of day. In the morning it had been downright cold, but by mid-afternoon it was almost hot whenever those windows of ever-shifting and towering cumulus clouds parted enough to let the sun burn through.

"He's walking up there, on Wayne," one of the women in the crowd shouted, before we could even get out of our cars. Off we drove, not knowing who or what we're looking for. About a quarter mile away on this tree lined, narrow, two-lane road we came across a man carrying a coat and walking away from us. He had a nasty gash on the back of his head and blood had stained his shirt collar. We hit the roof lights to warn traffic and got out to talk to him.

"What happened?" I asked.

"He hit me with a bottle, almost killed me."

"Who hit you?"

"The man back there at the store. He stole my money and hit me in the head."

"Is he still there?" I asked becoming embarrassed that one of us should have stayed at the store to begin the investigation.

"Yeah, he's still there."

"Do you want me to call the life squad?"

"No, no. I ain't going to no hospital."

My partner, sensing the back-up of traffic and realizing someone has to return to the store to investigate a possible armed robbery took control.

"Patrolman Klein, why don't you take the gentleman back to the station for a statement and I'll return to the scene of the crime."

The heavy set man, about 50 years old, and still clutching what appeared to be a thick winter coat, reluctantly made himself at ease in the front seat of my almost new 1971 Dodge patrol car. During the five minute ride to the station, and after advising the dispatcher of the situation, I made small talk trying to learn more about my passenger. Said he was retired, though he didn't look that old, and was living with his daughter in Lincoln Heights, an adjacent suburb.

Pulling into the station lot the radio broke squelch. I recognized my partner's identification as he broadcast, "Four-six-nine. Advise 4-6-8 his signal 22 is a signal 30. Request 4-8-4, signal 2, code 2 our office - assist 4-6-8."

My partner had told me the injured party was a wanted person and that it was serious enough that he was requesting assistance from another community! In retrospect, I guess I should have waited for the back-up to arrive. But hey, I was young and tough and besides the perp was already getting out of the scout car when the call came in.

Since he was bigger and he wasn't aware of his new status, I thought it might be better if we went inside. Entering the deserted squad room of the 1950's era police station, I ushered the perp to a chair on the pretext of wanting to apply first aid to his scalp wound. At the same time I began assuring him that we'd get the guy that attacked him.

Once seated, I knew the tactical position was mine. I reached for his coat that was now crumpled and lying on his lap while saying, "Let me take this. It will make you more comfortable, sir." As I pulled at the heavy wool material, I could now see the man's hand was wrapped around a revolver.

Instinctively I grabbed at it, he shoved at me with is left arm then everything seemed to be happening in slow motion. I could see my hand going for the perp's gun as the barrel slowly rotated toward me. I was trying to balance myself for the thrust of the perp's free elbow all the while my right hand raced to get at my service revolver. At the same time I was aware that my mind was screaming, why is it taking so long? My right hand clawed at the security strap on the Jordan holster. I seized the custom gripped three-fifty-seven magnum, again wondering why it was taking such an inordinate amount of time to clear leather. I heard my voice hollering, "LET GO! LET GO! LET GO!" I had what I hoped was a death grip on the gun-in-the-coat. The man was strong, I wasn't gaining an advantage, my Smith & Wesson started toward his throat, trigger finger tightening. The pending explosion of one or both weapons was imminent.

"LET GO! LET GO!" I knew as soon as my Model 19 reached battery it was going off. The magnum slammed into the perp's neck, my souped up mind was telling my unreasonably slow trigger finger: PULL, PULL, PULL.

The man relaxed, his gun hand released, he stopped shoving . . . and in that nano-second, through my mind flashed: kill him, he tried to kill you, they'll make you a hero, blow him away, kill him. But over-riding this subconscious speed-of-light musing was a deeper inner articulation: American police officer, fair play, the rule of law, the right thing to do.

By the time I had the assaulting weapon secured and was ordering the perp to lie face down on the floor the backup had arrived. We searched and cuffed him and threw him in the holding cell. My partner walked in as I began telling the sequence of events. He picked up the signal 30's revolver, opened it, looked at the loaded cylinder and said as he showed it to me, "you're a lucky guy."

The primer that had been under the hammer was dented - it had been struck by the firing pin. The man had pulled the trigger in an attempt to shoot me. But, because either the coat or my hand had impaired the fall of the hammer, it was a few ounces shy of striking hard enough to cause detonation.

I think it was then my knees got a little weak and angry thoughts of how this dirt bag had tried to kill me raced through my mind. This was followed by anger at myself for not blowing him away when I had the chance. If I had put the scum two-seven, I would be hailed a hero for taking a potential cop-killer off the streets and for surviving, for all intents and purposes, a firefight.

Turns out the perp, a walk-away from a mental hospital, had tried to steal goods from the food market and when confronted by the store owner, pulled the revolver on him. The proprietor, in self-defense, grabbed a pop bottle and hit the robber on the head. The store owner yelled for someone to call the police. A customer, who had only seen a bleeding man walking out of the store, called to report what she'd observed, merely, an "injured man."

There were no newspaper reports of the incident - like confrontations happen to police officers every day. My scrapbook doesn't contain any commendations of heroism, but I know, inside myself, I did the right thing and that's hero enough.

Chapter 6
HE SHOOT ME, TOO

It started out quiet enough for a Friday when my partner, John Campbell, and I began our Midnight to eight tour of duty. I was four-six-eight, the first-responder car, and John, the senior officer was car 4-6-9, the backup. We're police officers, our bailiwick is a small village adjacent to Cincinnati. Being a pint-sized community, we don't have the luxury of having our own dispatcher and thus rely on the County for all radio messages as did thirty-three other like towns and villages on the network. With this much radio traffic going through one dispatcher on one channel, all transmissions were on a very professional level with superfluous talk almost non-existent. To talk to another car or give detailed information to the dispatcher, the officers were to use the telephone, or if that was not practical, radio channel two could be used - but only with the dispatcher's permission.

The early part of the shift was consumed by checking the business areas and watching for drunk drivers with very little radio traffic, for us. The rest of the county was having a regular Friday night with many calls for bar fights, domestic trouble, and an occasional burglary report. About 2:00 AM, our quiet night became history as the dispatcher put out an all county broadcast with run-together-words and sentences only cops can decipher.

"Attention all cars all departments armed robbery just occurred the King Kwik Market Route 4 and Connersville Road Fairfield, wanted are three black male subjects wearing ski masks and armed with a sawed-off shotgun and blue steel revolver, last seen south bound State Route 4 in an older model Chrysler sedan, black-over-white in color, bearing Ohio six five three Charles David."

State Route 4 ran through the middle of our beat, and even though Fairfield was ten miles and one county north, I positioned myself at our northern boundary. After half an hour of waiting, I moved on, assuming the get-away car wasn't coming my way.

Soon the Dispatcher radioed our department to advise that the subject license was registered to a William Pilder of 11457 Shelter Road. That address was in our village and in a basically decent neighborhood. The Pilder family was not known as a harbor for criminals or trouble makers. Perhaps the person who copied the license number got it wrong – as often happens under stress.

My partner advised that since he was near the location, he'd check it out. I didn't hear anymore and when 4-6-9 and I met a little later he advised the Pilder place was a dark house on an empty driveway.

Back out on patrol I watched an older model black-over-white sedan approach me from the opposite direction on SR 4. I caught a glimpse of the license plate as we passed - it matched the one from the earlier broadcast and there were three occupants in the vehicle. As I started to turn my police-packaged Plymouth around, they took off at a high rate of speed. Fumbling, fighting, wrestling with the gear shift, steering wheel and emergency light/siren switch, I did my best to begin pursuit while keying the microphone:

"4-6-8, emergency traffic."

"All cars stand-by. 4-6-8, your emergency traffic."

"4-6-8 I'm in pursuit, black over white, Chrysler sedan bearing Ohio six, five, three, Charles David. We're south bound Route Four approaching Snyder Road. They've killed their lights"

"Okay 4-6-8. Four-six-eight are you aware these subjects possibly wanted armed robbery reference earlier broadcast?"

"4-6-8 affirmative. They're now running over 80."

"4-6-9, 4-1-7, 4-3-2, Four-six-eight in pursuit black over white Chrysler sedan south bound Route Four at Snyder. Subject vehicle believed wanted reference earlier broadcast for armed robbery. Be advised subject vehicle has no head lights."

My scout car was barely keeping up with the perps; I darted my eyes to the calibrated speedometer – 95! Then suddenly they slammed on their brakes and turned onto Rickman - a dead end residential street in a heavily wooded area.

"4-6-8 they just turned west on Rickman"

I knew the dispatcher and other cars heard me and were responding, but I was now totally focused on the Chrysler as it crested a small hill. Unexpectedly, the black over white slowed to a stop. The interior light briefly lit. The significance of this didn't register, though I slowed thinking perhaps they were going to run into the woods or make a stand. But the car took off again toward the dead end.

The Chrysler, having reached the road's limit, was now sliding to a halt. I locked the brakes up and cranked the wheel over hard to the left bringing the cruiser to a jolting stop abreast of the sedan. Training the spotlight on the perp's car, I opened my door, drew my service revolver just as the driver jumped out and made for the woods. Half laying over the windshield, I hollered as loud as I could, "FREEZE. DON'T MOVE." The man in the back seat quickly took my advice. My gut contracted and my arm muscles tensed as at any moment I expected to see muzzle flash from the woods.

Using the scout car as a shield, I began a series of shouted commands to try to control the situation. "ALL RIGHT NOW LISTEN UP. . .YOU, IN THERE . . . STICK YOUR HANDS OUT OF THE DOOR AND DON'T HAVE ANYTHING IN THEM. KEEP YOUR HANDS WHERE I CAN SEE THEM OR YOU'RE DEAD MEN."

All the while this was happening I knew the back-up cars were arriving by the sounds of their sirens, but split seconds seemed like hours. Upon my command only one man climbed out. Where was the third and where were the guns? I had the man out of the car and lying on the ground as the area filled with police cars in this normally quiet, dark, wooded, residential neighborhood. The robbers with the scattergun and handgun could be anywhere just waiting to blast any one of us at any moment. At times like this, the safety of the officers is primary to the rights of the suspects, so I knelt down next to the now handcuffed dude and placed my revolver at his head, saying, "If I or any other officer is shot by one of your buddies, I'm going to pull the trigger before I die . . . now tell me, where is the third guy and where are the guns?"

"He got out at the top of the hill – he took the shotgun."

"How 'bout the driver?"

"No. No. The handgun's in the back seat."

Quickly, I got on the PA and announced, "All units on the scene, there's two additional subjects in the woods - one armed with a shotgun."

Within minutes the canine unit from neighboring Blue Ash P.D. arrived and in short order found one of the missing robbers – the driver. The third man and the shotgun were still unaccounted for. The Chrysler was quickly searched, turning up only the blue steel revolver and a wallet, but no money. The wallet contained the identification of one Jerry Curtis, a two-time loser, who was out on parole for armed robbery!

The captured suspects were separated and transported to the station while LEOs from other departments inventoried the black over white sedan before having it towed to our impound lot.

Meanwhile at the station, the suspects, when confronted with the wallet, admitted to the robbery and that Curtis was the third man. They both stated Curtis had instructed the driver to stop just over the crest of the hill so he could get out, with the shotgun, and shoot the officer who was chasing them. Now it dawned on me why the interior light came on. I felt a chill at the visualization of the squad car window shattering as I took a full charge of buckshot. For whatever reason, he booked it into the woods letting his compatriots fend for themselves.

The driver, one Elliston Whitson, last known address, Chicago, was also on parole for armed robbery. The back seat man was Emanuel Pilder who had let Whitson drive the car belonging to Pilder's parents.

Jerry Curtis' parents lived within a mile of Rickman Road. Somewhere after 4:00 AM, with a couple of officers from an adjoining agency watching the back of the house, John and I rang the front door bell. A sleep-eyed Mrs. Curtis opened after we identified ourselves. We told her that the house was surrounded and that we believed her son Jerry had been involved in an armed robbery and we had come to arrest him. She said she was sure he was asleep in his upstairs bedroom as she had heard him come home a few hours ago. Mrs. Curtis then led us down the narrow, dimly lit hall to the stairs. I called up for Jerry to come down – twice. No response. Turning to Mrs. Curtis, I said, "You go up and get him." Her reply set my adrenaline flowing for the second time this night: "Hell's fire, I'm ain't goin' up there. He shoot me, too!"

Summoning all the authority I could in my voice, I hollered up the steps: "JERRY CURTIS, POLICE OFFICERS . . . IF YOU DON'T COME DOWN BY THE TIME I COUNT TO THREE, WE'RE COMING UP AFTER YOU. WE KNOW YOU HAVE A SHOTGUN AND THE HOUSE IS SURROUNDED . . . ONE . . . TWO . . . THREE. There was no sound or movement. John whispered to me, "You go high, I'll go low." I nodded. It was time to do what only police officers get paid to do.

With handguns at the ready, my gut squeezed tight yet again, I stepped around the corner and into that stairwell . . . prepared to shoot at anything that moved. Starting up the steps with the full expectation of gunfire, a resigned voice called out from above, "Don't shoot, I'm coming down."

By 6:00 a.m. it was all over, the vehicle impounded, the prisoners in lock-up and the paper work under control – time for a cup o' joe at the Country Kitchen. As I held the mug to warm my hands, I noticed they were shaking. Only then did I realize that I was scared. When it was happening – the chase, the confrontations, I didn't' have to time to think about what might happen. Now I had the shakes. The feelings of fear, which didn't last long, were a good sign because it made me appreciate life a little more.

Jerry Curtis and Elliston Whitson went back to prison for 10 to 20 stretches. Emanuel Pilder, due to his co-operation and no prior convictions, got probation. The money and shotgun have never been found.

Chapter 7
FROM THE OTHER SIDE OF THE BADGE

The sun has riz,
and the sun has set,
and we ain't outta Texas yet

The big square trademark radiator filled my outside rearview mirror. He looked like he was going to run over the top of me - and I was running 90 miles per hour! The dark blob in my mirror had been gaining on me for at least the past fifteen minutes. At first I thought it was a cop, but the rate he was closing was steady and not increasing as if it were the police. Besides, 90 was not really considered speeding west of San Antonio. Speed limit signs were seldom encountered and actual "speed limits" in many parts of the west were whatever was "reasonable and proper."

I had left Houston early that morning with limited funds advanced by the Show Winds Theatrical Company. It was late May, 1961, I was nineteen and had started a dream summer vacation job as the front man for a live stage show company that produced one-night stands in small towns across the southwest. My first scheduled stop-over was Pecos.

I edged closer to the berm and again checked my instruments: Tach, 4000, engine temperature 185°F, oil pressure . . . . It was a huge silver and black Rolls Royce and it was now abreast of me. The mustachioed driver, black cap atop his head, didn't even acknowledge me while the passenger, in the rear seat, couldn't be seen from behind the newspaper he was reading.

This is not happening. This is Texas, USA, and I'm driving the most powerful American made car - the 1960 Corvette! I can't let this happen - this is for the honor of America. I fed a little more fuel to my three Rochester, two-barrel carburetors and matched the interlopers speed - 110.

After a few minutes in his slipstream, I moved over into the east bound lanes and shoved my foot in it. The little roadster responded with push-you-back-in-the-seat acceleration while the twin straight-thru mufflers resonated off the side of the Rolls. I topped out at a little over 125 and then settled back to 120 - a nice easy two-mile-per-minute clip. I gleefully watched the Rolls growing smaller in my mirrors.

It was hot, maybe 95 or so, and even the rush of air at such a high speed didn't help much. My cheerfulness quickly faded upon glancing at my gauges. The engine temperature was approaching 220 degrees! I had been running all day at 90 without straining the engine, but the extra 30 MPH had been too much. I cut back down to 90. Sure enough, 15 minutes later here came the Rolls with the haughty chauffeur and oblivious passenger; 110, steady as she goes. Well, we don't have to tell anyone - obviously they won't - they didn't even know they had slighted an American icon.

Hot, dirty and tired I found a cabin at Jim Bob's & Mary Beth's Tourist Haven just outside Pecos. The sign said free TV and air-conditioning. After checking in, I discovered the free amenities were only available in the office. Eight hours of sleep and I was ready to begin work. The agreement was; I was to deliver and post bills in common places of the city. I was also to visit any and all local radio stations and newspapers with publicity releases and offer interviews. Posting the flyers was without incident. However, the radio stations and the only local newspaper were reluctant to give me an interview or a promise to plug the upcoming show – seems they had heard my company's song before.

I was allowed two days to complete my work before moving on to the next municipality. At each town the Company was to have waiting for me a money order, care of general delivery. On the morning of the third day there was still no letter at the post office. I called Houston and was told some long tale that I should not worry they'll make it up to me in Farmington, New Mexico, the next stop on the list. Boy, was I naive. The company hadn't sent me out completely without support. They had given me $30.00 for gas money, which, at .20/gallon was good for about 800 miles.

Around noon the next day, I rolled into Roswell just as a local parade was mustering on the main drag. I flopped the top and, hand waving to the crowds like I was one of the floats, got into line behind what turned out to be the mayor's car - a '61 Chevy Convertible. About the time the parade got to the center of town, a motorcycle cop pulled alongside, signaling that I should follow him. Oops. At the police station, I tried to tell them I was just following traffic when I somehow got mixed up with the parade vehicles. That was almost truthful inasmuch as a cop, way back at the beginning, asked me if I was in the parade and I nodded yes. Since they couldn't get the mayor to forgo his parade and ceremonial affair to hear my case, the sergeant ordered that I be escorted out of town. Sometimes ya get lucky. Now I was on my way to Route 66 and Albuquerque for dinner and a night's sleep.

The next day, I gassed up and inquired of the best route to Farmington. The locals at the gas station, while admiring my car and asking if I was on the Route 66 TV show, advised I should stay on 66 to Gallup and turn north there as the state roads running out of Albuquerque to the four-corners area were not all paved. I didn't tell them I was on the show, but I didn't tell them I wasn't, either. On my way out of town, I noticed I had picked up a few followers - kids from the gas station who had tried to goad me into a race. The leader of the pack; driving a maroon 1959 Chevrolet with louvers on the hood, lowering blocks and a shaved nose and deck, kept riding up on my rear bumper. Once or twice, when traffic permitted, he pulled alongside, shoved it into second gear and goosed it a few times while his shotgun called for a race. After a few miles of this, the taunts and threats became abusive and it was clear I needed to do something.

Picking a stretch of U.S. 66 that looked to have a sharp curve with a clear view at the end of a short straightaway, I changed down into third and opened the throttle full. The '59, taken by surprise, lagged a hundred feet back by the time I had entered the hard right hand turn. One of the other attributes I added to my Vette was a panel that included switches for my brake lights, tail lights, left tail light, four-way-flasher (not a factory option yet) and under-hood lights. The tail light switch was in case I was being followed at night, by someone I didn't want to catch me - such as a cop. I could turn out the tail lights making it very hard for him to see me. The left tail light switch was for the same purpose, whereas if a cop was chasing a car with two tail lights, but after a few hills and dales, the only car in front of him had one tail light, he would think the car he was chasing had turned off. It did work, but that's another story.

Hurtling down the highway at close to 90, and with the '59 coming on strong, things got very busy. Just before trouncing the binders, I flipped the switch cancelling the brake lights. With a quick heal-toe maneuver I jammed the shift lever into second gear red-lining the engine. The car shuttered as the speed dropped. Tires howling in protest, I induced an under-steer setting up a four wheel drift. As the right front tire, just over the edge of the pavement and on the dirt berm fought for adhesion, and immediately before the apex, I poured the coal to her while straightening the wheel to compensate for drift. Once clear of the corner, I stole a glance at my rear view mirror. The Chevy driver, obviously thinking that if I could take the corner without braking, he could too - learned too late something wasn't right. I couldn't see exactly what happened, but there was a lot of dust and I never saw them again.

Farmington was void of any hotels or motels, but I did find a nice home that offered rooms to rent; $3.00 per night including breakfast and dinner. That was after I checked the post office - no mail here either. I couldn't help being an optimist; my mother was a Pollyanna. I began the next day calling on the local radio station. Here, a kindly, older DJ/station manager took pity on me and told me last year, after the town had been excited about and helped promote the theatrical company - they never showed up. When I told him of how I hadn't been paid he offered to treat me to dinner at his lodge in Durango, Colorado.

The trip through the mountains to this old west town, nestled down into a valley amid jagged mountain peaks, was the most beautiful scenery I had ever seen. The "one dog" town was right out of a Louis L'Amour dime novel as was the rustic Moose Lodge, complete with hand hewn, exposed rafters and, of course, a giant moose head mounted over a huge stone fireplace. The western attired members, in their scuffed boots and sweat-stained hats, were authentic, not fancy fringed-shirted Hollywood cowboy wannabees.

Arriving back in Farmington, I found a parking ticket on my windshield. It seemed that everywhere I went, cops were attracted to my Corvette. Not, I'm sure, as enthusiasts, but because they assumed sooner or later the driver was going to race, speed, spin his tires, make noise or all of the above. Their concerns were not without merit. The $3.00 ticket became $100.00 if not paid within 24 hours. Twenty-four or a thousand hours, I wasn't about to pay it. It wasn't the principle of the thing, I just didn't have three bucks to spare!

Early the next morning, I headed for the post office. That was, of course, after I paid my room bill and had a full breakfast. The matronly, middle aged, everybody's-mom-lady-of-the-house, in her gingham dress, wished me good luck. The postmaster advised the mail truck wasn't due for about an hour. I walked to the corner drug store, ordered a coke at the soda fountain and read a three-day old copy of the local paper.

The mail contained nothing for me. Then it was back to the drug store where I used the pay phone to place a collect call to the producer. He refused my call! Well, at least I got gas money to get me this far. California here I come.

As I hit the town's western limit the red light on the police car that had been following me came on. I stopped, got out and walked back to the cruiser.

"You gonna pay that ticket, boy," the rotund, red-faced cop spat.

"Not right now, sir. But I will."

"Looks to me like you're leaving town - and that's another crime iffins you gotta outstanding ticket."

"Uh, no sir. I was just going to run a mile or two on the highway. My plugs were beginning to foul from all that town driving I'd been doing and I thought I'd blow 'em out a little. I can't leave until I do the radio interview tonight," I lied.

"Well, you go ahead, but if you ain't back in ten minutes, I'm gonna radio to Shiprock to stop you and lock you up. Ya hear?"

It was 25 miles to Shiprock and then another 20 to the Arizona border. Approaching the turn-off to this final town, at my normal 4000 RPM cruising speed of 90, I could see two police cars, lights flashing, blocking the right lane. A uniformed officer was standing in the middle of the road, his hand held up, palm forward. I slowed to about 35, shifted to 2nd to wait for the on-coming pickup truck to clear the road block. With the left lane now open, I moved across the yellow line as the officers began waving their hands and shouting. I had to put two wheels on the dirt shoulder to keep from hitting them as they watched, dumbfounded, America's only real sports car rocket away from them. It was a gamble, but I figured the chances of another cop being between me and the border to be slim. Lucky again!

****

Seeing her at her Mother's funeral forced memories forever melded to the sentimental portions of my mind.

```````````````````

In my 13th year, the summer of 1954, the Cooper's moved next door. I was just starting to notice girls and Suzan – Suzie - got my attention when she beat me at a game of mumbly-peg. And, even though she was a tom-boy, she was a very good looking tom-boy. Nothing was ever said, but my best friend, Carl, knew that the looks between her cyan and my hazel eyes meant a destiny that didn't include him. Our families became close in many ways. Suzie and I were the same age, her brother and I swam on the school team together and our mothers became the very best of friends.

Throughout high school, I was on the wild side - a hot rodder - and only dated "chicks." I was embarrassed to call Suzie until I'd sowed my oats. I re-noticed her when she came over to swim late in the summer of '61. Now, I was enrolled in college and more mature - and she was so pretty. Somehow I talked her into a date for that Saturday night. I then spent an entire day cleaning and polishing my 1960 Corvette. The Vette was rigged for road racing with the quick-steering adapter, HD shocks, metallic brake linings and 3" x 6" galvanized pipe welded to the exhaust header
```````````````````

pipes. The only external change to the car was the addition of Marchal head lamps to replace the outboard standard sealed beam lights.

Temperature wise, it was a perfect Cincinnati evening and I had the top down and soft music playing on the RCA 45 record player I had installed on the "chicken bar" ('cuz the radio was all static due to the solid spark plug wires). She wore something white and was so pretty – wait, I already said that. Slowly, so as to enjoy the music and not disturb her with the loud exhaust, we motored to Sorrento's restaurant, turning every head we passed. Though Corvettes weren't common and car aficionados would always look, everyone noticed a beautiful blonde.

We spent a lot of time together that late summer – swimming, dancing, movies and other fun stuff. One warm night, while watching an Elvis Presley movie at the drive-in, The King sang "Can't Help Falling In Love." At the line, "Take my hand, take my whole life too . . . ." we instinctively reached to hold hands. I don't remember the song being "our song," but whenever I've heard it, I've thought of Suzie. The end of September found her returning to the University of Colorado at Boulder and our courtship continued via mail.

In mid January, exams over and during a conversation with my friend and fellow hot rod club member, Kookie, I suggested we run out to Boulder. He didn't have anything else going on and was game, especially after I promised Suzie would fix him up with a real honey.

We picked up U.S. 36 in downtown Indianapolis, a reprieve, after following mostly state highways with their inherent undulations, stream-chasing routes and long, wild grasses growing over the edge of the pavement (expressways yet to open). West of the city the traffic thinned out and we were able to return to our cruising speed of 90 MPH. The Corvette had three Rochester 2-barrel carburetors on straight linkage and at that speed the engine was running 4000 RPM which was well into the power curve of the Duntov cam. In other words, it was a comfortable clip that produced over 14 miles per gallon.

Somewhere around 5:00 a.m., in a dense fog, a wheel came off. Kookie was driving and did a great job of keeping the Vette on the road. There was no damage to the car, but, due to the thick fog we never found the tire and wheel. We took a lug nut from each of the other wheels and used those three nuts to hold the spare tire on. Limping into the next town we found a Chevrolet dealer and after a two hour wait for them to open, we were on our way again.

Deep into western Kansas, running the usual 90 per, a semi-truck emerged about a half mile ahead. It appeared we would pass the truck, maintaining the present rate, in the middle of an intersection. The land was flat and the cross road was clear, so I just held her steady at 4000 RPM. Halfway around the semi and over the double yellow line, I was startled to see a state trooper on the truck's front bumper! The noise from the muffler by-pass reverberating off the truck was deafening and produced a look of surprised outrage on the trooper's face as we roared past. Not for an instant did I think I could talk my way out of speeding, excessive noise, driving left of center and passing in an intersection.

I went to full throttle while Kookie scanned the map. One Hundred . . . a hundred and ten . . . two-miles-per-minute. We were a lightning bolt on wheels. My co-pilot leaned over and shouted that there was only one little town and then about ten miles to Colorado. We had to chance that there weren't any other cops between us and the border. Now my attention was riveted to controlling this 300 horse-powered, plastic-bodied roadster – a land-rocket that was sans power brakes, power steering or steel-belted-radial-tires. At these speeds even glancing at the gauges was forsaken. I had to rely on engine sounds, the feel of the wheel, gut instincts and luck. Billboards and highway signs such as Burma-Shave and Mail Pouch became mere peripheral splashes of color.

Coming into the small burg, a pandemonium of smoke and danger - fire shooting from the open lake-pipes - people stopped and stared, mouths agape. I forced the Vette to just under 60 in second gear to negotiate a hard left turn then got a piece of third before having to shut down for a tight chicane in the heart of town. Once through the business district, I red-lined in third gear before leveling off again at 90. The state trooper was nowhere in sight.

Inside Colorado, with Denver in view, we came around a bend in the road and there sat two highway patrol cars. Both pulled out after us. We got out of their sight over a small hill and slammed to a stop. Having anticipated this from previous high speed runs, Kookie and I were both wearing like-colored shirts. When the officers finally pulled up behind us, we were standing outside the car studying a road map. They couldn't give us a ticket, because they were unable to determine who was driving. However, they let us know that Kansas had called that we were coming and they were going to follow us all the way through their state if necessary. They stayed with us until we turned off at Boulder.

At the university, we found a motel and called Suzie. She came right over and the hug and kiss made it all worthwhile. We got a little shut-eye, Suzie came through with a co-ed for Kookie and we did the college scene. The next day, Kookie wanted to see a mountain and the girls found the way, where we took pictures and enjoyed the day.

The home-bound leg was uneventful except for the final stretch in Indiana . . . where on lazy, sunny, summer days giant deciduous trees over-hang the country roadways, their branches reaching out as if to shake hands. Uneventful: except this was night, the dead of winter and we picked up a cop. I quickly tripped the switch I had installed to cancel the left tail light. A few miles further down this highway that snaked in and out of those towering trees and the officer, who had been chasing two tail lights, now only saw a vehicle with one light and surely figured we turned at a side road – which he must have done as we never saw him again.

The trip out took almost 24 hours due to losing the tire. Coming back, we covered the 1190 miles in 19 hours, five minutes - a 63 MPH average - all on two lane roads with no side-lines and very narrow, if any, shoulders. I've never been sure the trip wasn't more about the opportunity to road race than it was to see my girl.

I developed some very strong feelings for her and I know she pined for me also, but the timing wasn't right. Both of us had agendas - places to go, things to do, worlds to conquer and commitments were a long way off.

It is said that everyone experiences three loves: the one they marry, the one they're glad they didn't marry and the one that got away

Suzie and I kept in touch, but with careers and dating others the touch got lighter. Within a few years, Suzan accepted a job in California and . . . married. Me? As soon as I figured out that it was just as much fun to be the chaser as it was the chasee, I became a police officer.

The Corvette? A few months after the Colorado trip, before I burned the valves experimenting with nitro-methane and sold it to an unsuspecting dealer, I made one last run. They had just opened the six-lane Interstate between Cincinnati and Dayton and nine of us, all in Corvettes - three rows of three - broke in the new road. With seven Vettes to block cops, two at a time would line up, and from a roll, run flat out. I was up against a '59 270 with a higher rear axle ratio. I beat him from 70 to about 130, and then he came on by.

Yeah, I know, we were crazy back then. But traffic was light, cops fewer, radar not perfected and we were very lucky. Lucky to survive and lucky to have lived during that era.

Late in the spring of 1996, and now a widower, my second wife, Annette, and I were honored to be treated to lunch with Mrs. Cooper and my mother. Suzie, who has known Annette since grade school, was in town for a visit and also joined us. Both of my wives have known about "Suzie and me." I made certain they did - a tinge of jealousy never hurt any relationship. I always wondered if Suzan, in the same vein, kept Paul on his toes, too.

Never being able to satiate aspirations
is better than not having
any fantasies at all.

At some point during the luncheon, Suzie and I found ourselves alone . . . and 42 years since our eyes locked in that game of mumbly-peg, I asked this girl next door, "Did life turn out okay? Are you happy?" She smiled, her blue eyes twinkling, "Oh yes. Surely you remember your mother always telling us, 'the secret to life is the ability to adapt to change.' And you?" I smiled out of the corner of my mouth and gave her a slow wink, "Can't argue with my mom."

~~~~~~~~~~~~~~~~

After the funeral Suzan introduced me to her
daughters, one of which immediately turned to her sisters
and whispered, "He's Klein. He could have been our
father."

Chapter 8
THE SEVENTH SENSE

(Author's note: Though technically not a "story" this article illustrates the mind set of what it takes to be an LEO.)

PREFACE:

Are police officers any different from anyone else? Can any Jane or Joe be an LEO? Oh sure, we hear that all cops have a 6th sense – the real or perceived ability to tell when something's not right or when the interviewee is lying. The 6th sense does exist and is an important asset. However, it's not mandatory that all police officers have it. Some cops can remember names and faces while others never forget a license plate number or vehicle description. Different attributes are necessary to be able to relate to many peoples and conditions. For example, Mutt and Jeff teams of bad cop – good cop are notorious for working a confession out of a perp.

But the real difference, the trait that sets the Jane and Joes from the LEOs apart is the 7th sense – the inborn and intrinsic sense of right and wrong. Like its cousin, the 6th, it can't be learned. You either are of high moral and ethical nature or you're not. Unfortunately, this isn't something that can be determined exclusively by examination. Background checks, written and verbal tests coupled with personal interviews help predict whether the shield will tarnish or shine, but it's usually the agency head that must use his or her 6th sense to determine who has the 7th sense and will make an honest cop.

The threat of terrorist strikes and the new Homeland Security demands are putting increasing pressure on America's first line of defense. Not only do they now have to continue to deal with the common criminal, handle domestic disputes, traffic accidents and other "regular" duties, but the new level of possible massive attacks is heavy on the mind. However, and this is a big however, the beat cops must not - regardless of the pressure - forsake their duty to adhere to their sworn obligations. No matter what the provocation or public opinion American police officers must remain true to their primary responsibility to protect the citizenry - including even the most reprehensible of perps. Part of this sworn duty includes maintaining the highest level of ethical behavior and the commitment to put one's self in harm's way if called upon to do so.

USE OF DEADLY FORCE:

Police officers carry firearms and less-than-lethal tools for two reasons: 1) For purposes of self-protection and, 2) To protect society. Ergo, since society allows police to carry these defensive instruments to facilitate the requisites of the job, it goes without saying that officers are expected to place themselves between danger and members of society when so required.

With the best of intentions some police trainers, in an attempt to save officer's lives, have been teaching a mind-set that equates to protect yourself first. Their mantra is - don't take chances - suicide is not in your job description.

A MATTER OF SEMANTICS:

Perhaps one of the problems is the definitions of words or phrases. Some have interpreted the notion that "police officers should never act in a cowardly manner" to mean cops must sacrifice their lives for the sake of not being labeled chicken. Nothing could be further from the truth. There is a difference between sacrifice/suicide (purposely giving up one's life to save another) and duty (complying with a moral or legal obligation related to one's occupation or position). An officer's life is of no greater or lesser value than that of any other citizen. However, because of their unique duty, they have agreed, by a sworn oath, to place their life - but not to the point of surrender - at risk. In a timely manner and short of sacrifice, a police officer is duty bound to place her life in jeopardy to protect members of society.

No one is saying or expecting an LEO to sacrifice his life, but each officer has the duty to protect the public. The very nature of the police occupation is centered on dangerous activity. If the work involved only taking reports, directing traffic and calling in a SWAT team when danger appears, the job could be done by social workers or clerks.

Being afraid is okay. Perhaps the best definition of overcoming fear to perform one's duty is found in the plot and theme song to the early 1950s movie, *High Noon.* Here, on his wedding day, the town Marshall (played by Gary Cooper) learns a man he sent to prison is returning on the noon train. The officer is torn between leaving on his honeymoon, as planned, or staying to face the perp. His bride (played by Grace Kelly) begs her groom to give it up. She leaves without him as Tex Ritter wails the theme song - the watchwords of police officers of all time:

> "*I do not know what fate awaits me,*
> *I only know I must be brave,*
> *for I must face the man who hates me,*
> *or lie a coward,*
> *a craven coward,*
> *or lie a coward in my grave.*"

The bride returns just in time to blow one of the gang members away to save her man, who then out-draws the ex-con. In real life, sometimes the perp wins and sometimes the spouse doesn't come back. But to a sworn police officer either one of those conditions is preferable than being labeled a craven coward.

TYPES OF OFFICERS:

When it comes to dealing with dangerous situations, there tends to be three types of police officers: Fool, Coward and Hero. Fortunately, the hero type overwhelmingly represents the American police ranks. In a small, dangerous minority are the others.

THE FOOL:

The Fool is one who tempts fate by ignoring training procedures and expertise such as not wearing body armor or, for example, not calling for backup when stopping an armed robbery suspect. While apprehension of criminals is an end in and of itself, per se, only a fool attempts a collar at the expense of officer safety. However, that is not to say that anything short of sacrificing one's life in order to protect/save the life of one you are sworn to serve and protect is not part of the job. This is also not to say that bravado is the same as bravery. There is a difference.

COWARD TYPES:

The Coward is one who fails to institute a serious attempt to protect society due to fear or a mindset that equates personal safety over the moral and legal obligation to protect others. Any officer failing to place himself in harm's way because of such an attitude is guilty of non-feasance at best or malfeasance at worst. A coward is also one who flat-out ignores suspicious activity in order to avoid dangerous confrontations. One of the duties of an FTO is to weed cowards out of the ranks. Of course, if the FTO is a coward . . . .

In response to an article on this subject, one police chief wrote: "Most officers are just like everyone else. Their main goal is to get home safely at the end of each shift." Wrong! Police officers are not "just like everyone else" they are the only ones with a sworn duty to protect "everyone else".

"[T]o get home safely" might be a great concept for sanitation workers or lawyers, but contrary to what this public official espouses, the "main goal" of a police officer should be to serve and protect the public.

There is no mandate that any officer should be expected to sacrifice her life, but it does mean there are certain inherent risks that come with the badge and take precedent over the desire "to get home safely". U.S. Secret Service agents' main goal, as we have seen in notorious film clips, is to protect the protectee even if it means using their own bodies as a shield. Should they not do so to insure that they can go home at night? Where would we be, if for the same self-serving reasons, American soldiers had forsaken their duty to engage the enemy during past wars? To put it on a more personal level; suppose you're caught in a firefight - what main goal would you expect of your backup?

A police officer who doesn't believe that cowardice is a fate worse than death, is in the wrong business.

The standard that one may use deadly force if one believes he is about to be the victim of a lethal force assault is well established in law. This doctrine of self defense applies to cops as well as civilians. Of course, this belief must be based upon something other than pure fear, such as the perp has a gun or a knife. Even then, being afraid the perp might use the weapon is not sufficient. There must be some overt action or non-action such as refusing to drop the weapon that can only be interpreted as life threatening and immediate. Unleashing a hail of hollow-points without those qualifying conditions is the mark of a coward.

HERO TYPES:

Ordinarily, in the presence of danger, most citizens become excited as their blood pressure rises and fear registers. Contrarily, the heroic type, when facing confrontational perils, tends to experience a stabilization of vital signs and a calming effect as discipline, training and faith in themselves takes hold.

The Hero is one who realizes an officer's primary duty is to protect and serve the public. This American idol firmly believes he would rather be a dead hero than a live coward and would shun another officer who acted in a cowardly manner. However, this officer is not the fool inasmuch as she learns and practices safe tactics and procedures. American policing is the standard of the world, the epitome to which all others aspire. We didn't get that way by unilaterally changing the rules of engagement for egocentric rationality.

Except to those who like to make excuses, there is not a fine line between when prudence becomes cowardice or bravado. An officer advised of a man brandishing a gun in a school should request immediate backup and then, without hesitation, proceed into the building. His goal is to find and end the risk. Anything less is cowardice, non-feasance and against all of what America stands for. On the other hand, if the officer is advised of a bank robbery in-progress, rushing in might be a foolish move. But, not placing oneself in a position to engage the suspects upon their exiting the bank - even before backup arrives - would certainly be deemed cowardice. Likewise, if a crazed gunman opens fire in a shopping mall, public square or school duty demands drawing fire away from the unarmed civilians.

The prudent-heroic persona should be the ultimate goal for officers. One can teach prudence to the heroic type person, but not the reverse. Heroism, like cowardice, is intrinsic and not readily learned – a 7th sense. Self-preservation is inherent in all humans, though, unlike cowardice, it is not over-riding to the heroic type. Teaching self-preservation as a primary function goes against the grain of the heroic type.

THE MAIN ISSUE - TRAINING:

Training, be it class room or on the street, begets predictable behavioral results. All officers must prove to their fellow officers that they are not cowards - that they can be counted on to help a fellow officer under any and all circumstances. Cops must never hesitate to jump into a melee lest they be branded a coward. Civilians, for the most part, are thankful for this machismo as this is what compels cops to risk their lives to protect civilians. Besides, if you were a cop would you want a partner that was afraid to jump into a fisticuff to save your backside?

However, there have been far too many well-documented (some on video tape) Rodney King type beatings. These modern day "blanket parties" are acts of cowardice - actions of police officers who are in reality, cowards, trying to prove their manhood by acting aggressively when there is no chance they will be hurt. Beating the stuffing out of some murderous scumbag might be the only punishment the perp will receive, but it is not, under any standard, an act of bravery. Besides, as justifiable as it might seem, police are only empowered to apprehend criminals - not inflict retribution.

MENTAL BRAVERY:

This text book ethics stuff is all well and good, but what happens in real life when a sworn police officer witnesses a fellow officer violate the law. Does she arrest the offender? Tattle-tale to the supervisor? Adhere to the "code of blue silence?" Used to be the answer was: "It depends on the infraction." If the violation wasn't something major, like a class A felony, and the public hadn't witnessed it, then it was kept quiet or it was left up to a ranking officer. Problem was, just where do you draw the line? What infractions are reportable? Petty theft? Perjury? DUI? Violating a citizen's civil rights because he spit on you? Turning your back, averting your eyes, not volunteering information are all acts of cowardice.

When it comes to police deviance there are two factors that determine the level of compliance: Peer pressure and trust. Peer pressure dates to grade school and is reprehensible when practiced by trained, sworn police officers who, by their very job description, are individuals. A person who is so mentally weak - cowardly - that he is compelled to go along with the illegal activities of others of her group, is not qualified to wear a badge. It's one thing for a bunch of civilians to sneak off the work detail for a beer and an entirely different matter for professional - armed - officers to do the same.

No lying, no cheating, no stealing. No exceptions, no excuses.

Trust in the form of reliance is sometimes difficult to differentiate from trust in the sense of confidentiality. Confidentiality belongs to the "you ain't dirt if you're not a cop," "good ol' boy," "blue code of silence" schools. Not conducive to professional stature, this type of trust falsely conveys a belief that if an officer "covers-up" or keeps quiet about improper activity he can be trusted as backup when things get really scary. Any professional who stakes her reputation on keeping his mouth shut when she is under a sworn oath not to, is not worthy of the honor of being one of "America's finest." Second, any officer staking his back-up support on a partner who supports the confidentiality mind-set may wind up dead.

Trust in the form of reliance, on the other hand, is of extreme importance to the functioning of any police agency. Cops, being individualists, sometimes need unquestioning reliance from their fellow officers. When an officer's back is exposed during a lethal force or other dangerous situation, this officer needs to know that his partner, his backup, can be counted on to defend her to the death. Being the kind of officer who has mastered the "code of blue silence" is not any indication of how that officer will respond under conditions of extreme stress. The only sure method of determining trust by reliance is the oldest application of trial by fire. On the other hand, an officer who is known for his unquestioning honesty would be the type of officer who couldn't honestly not take risks to cover your backside.

> *The American Police Officer: A balance of benevolence to the community with enforcement of the law, in concert to the Constitution, all the while adhering to highest moral and ethical ideals.*

A few years ago when cops were underpaid, undereducated and selected more for brawn than mental capacity, a certain amount of "discretion" was expected. Not today. Patrol officers routinely earn a decent living wage, have excellent health care packages and retirement plans that customarily exceeds the general population. The substantial amount of on-going training, education and certification police officers receive has elevated their status from that of tradesmen to the level of professional. All professionals have a code of ethics. A doctor will not treat the patient of another physician unless referred and an attorney won't have direct contact with clients of other lawyers. The cop's stock-in-trade is honesty and integrity - he must, above all, not compromise these.

An officer who acts as a coward by adhering to the code of blue silence to cover-up the illegal, unethical and/or immoral behavior of a fellow officer must be removed from office.

Police officers are in the business of honesty. This is their stock-in-trade, forte', signature, persona, identification and what differentiates them from other professions. When one police officer violates this trust, this code of honesty, all are tarnished. Adherence to or practice of any form of "blue code of silence" is counter to the code of honesty that is part of each officer's sworn duty - his existence for being. The trust each officer has in her fellow officer must be based on the proposition that truth, not cover-up or silence, will save his career. For a police officer or anyone with sworn obligations, justice is more important than friendship.

SUMMARY:

The terroristic assaults of 9-11-01 evidenced true acts of heroism. In a feature article in Smithsonian Magazine (September 2002), two naval officers, ". . . turned against the flow of people fleeing to safety and headed toward what appeared to be the point of greatest destruction." At risk to their own personal safety and though severely injured, these officers were responsible for saving lives. This is what America is all about - duty and honor in the face of death.

Police officers, who possess the 7th sense will never stray from the protect the public first standard and accept the reality that placing oneself in harm's way and sticking to the truth regardless of the consequences is part of the job. As the entire country prepares for the certainness of future terroristic attacks we must be secure in our persons and places that America's Finest will not ignore their heroic duties and always act in the most ethical of ways. If America's first line of defense fails this simple edict, America and the American police profession are lost.

Chapter 9
SOMETIMES YA GET LUCKY

Convertibles are great, sports cars even better, but best for pure motoring fun is a motorcycle - and a Harley Davidson is the most fun of all. Decked out in torn, ragged denim work pants and a sleeveless shirt, Sander Rackman looked and felt like a hardened outlaw biker as he followed the old highway to Warsaw, deep in the mountainous hills and valleys of Kentucky.

"Hi. Where can I find Eve?"

The bag boy glanced around while bagging groceries for a matronly looking farmer's wife who covered Sander with a disdainful stare.

"I'm not sure. I don't think she comes in 'till eleven. Ask the manager - he's over there," the kid said, nodding toward the bread racks.

Eleven it is. Maybe a cup of coffee at the Bun Boy across the street and a few phone calls will help kill some time. Rackman had gotten a tip that the target's girl friend, Eve, worked at this IGA. The target was the guy named in the summons in Sander's pocket. The client was a knockout of a lady lawyer. He wasn't privy to particulars of the case; his job was to serve process.

A few minutes before the hour he parked his Hog in the back of the IGA lot where employees would usually park, sat on the ground leaning against the MC and watched. The bike fit Sander's image: scruffy and rough - not some shiny, primped sissified bad-boy-wannabe's ride. Right on time an old beater with a woman driver, you could hardly call her a chick, drove in and parked two spaces to his left. Take away the clean, starched uniform and she'd look like she'd seen a few too many miles from the back of Harley.

"Hey, Eve baby, how ya doin'? It's Char," Sander said to her quizzical frown. Making up stuff as he went along in hopes of gaining her trust, he continued, "You know, we met up at the Roundup a while back. I'm looking for your old man. Where can I find him?"

With her lip twisted and a squint, she replied, "Char? Wasn't you at the pig roast up to Cecil's place back a couple of months ago?"

"Yeah, I was there too. But I thought I also saw you at the Roundup," he ad-libbed.

"Look, I'm gonna be late for work, ah what . . . ."

"I was just wondering where I can find your old man."

"First off, I ain't got no old man no more, and second, I don't know, much less care where the hell he is. Nice bike you got."

With the knowledge that she and Knueson were on the outs he put on his best smile. "Well, if you ain't seein' him no more maybe you and I could toss a few down sometime."

She turned toward him thrusting her hip out, "Yeah, maybe we could at that . . . Char. Why don't you stop back around nine when I get off work?"

"I can't tonight baby. But ah, I'd like to take a rain check. Where can I find Bobby? He promised to put me on to his main man."

"Have you tried his farm? And he ain't got a main man. He's the main man if you catch my drift. He grows the stuff his self right there. But don't tell him I told ya or he'll kill me. Know what I mean, honey? The farm is down around Bee Camp Hollar - over to Switzerland County. The name on the mailbox is the name William Cusper - that's the name he uses."

She smiled through chipped, nicotine stained teeth as the P.I. smiled back thinking he wouldn't' take her to a dog fight – even if she was fighting.

Some clouds, along with the humidity, had begun to roll in, but as long as he kept the older model FLH moving, it was comfortable enough. At the only gas station in town he learned that Switzerland County was right across the dam bridge in Indiana. It took a stop at the Vevay police department to learn the location of Bee Camp Hollar and that William R. Cusper was only known as such. A check at the courthouse provided the information that a William Cusper did in fact own 178 acres on Bee Camp plus another 40 in Posey Township. Neither of the properties were encumbered by any liens. There was no record of Bobby Knueson. The man might be a drug manufacturing, biker-sleeze bag, but he was smart enough to keep his real identity secret to the locals. Even though the subpoena in his pocket only had the name of Bobby Knueson, it would still be good as long as he added the a.k.a.

The hollar looked just like the name sounded - down-home, unsophisticated good 'ol boy country. The rusty mailbox with the crudely hand painted name, Cusper, was perched atop an old stump. The farm house, if you could call it that, was visible back a short gravel drive. The house was really an older double-wide that could use a little sprucing up. A polished Harley Sportster and a dusty, but well cared for, late model Ford F-150 pick-up truck were parked off to the side and in front of a weathered, wood-sided barn.

Sander secured his bike near the mailbox and walked to the trailer. The door was standing open so he called, then yelled for Mr. Cusper. Dirty dishes were scattered throughout the kitchen and living room as were articles of clothing, beer cans and an empty pizza box. What really caught his attention was the AR15 or M16 rifle, he couldn't tell which, and handfuls of ammunition lying on the stained, sun faded sofa.

The barn was also void of any living creatures, disturbingly quiet save for the sound of a tractor. He walked in the direction of the noise which came from around back of the barn and a stand of cedars. In the adjoining field was a man on a red and silver trimmed Massey Ferguson diesel tractor pulling a sixty-inch bush-hog. The operator, a man of about forty, throttled back as Sander approached. Above the din of the tractor and rotating blades he shouted, "William Cusper?"

"Yeah, what do you want?" the man hollered back. He was a burly man with large, dark eyes and curly, black hair that was matted with sweat. On his upper arm was the tattoo of an eagle. He pulled a blue bandanna from a hip pocket and wiped a neck that was as thick as a tractor tire.

Producing the court paper from a back pocket, Sander handed it to Cusper, saying, "Thanks, you've been served."

Before he could back away, the man shoved it back shouting, "I ain't Mr. Cusper. I thought you was ah askin' if this was his place. He's gone for now but will be back around sundown."

Since Sander didn't have any physical description of the man and no other way to identify him, he had to take the subpoena back or risk a bad service. Before he could ask any more questions the tractor had been set into motion again, forcing him to step out of the way.

Serving process was always an iffy proposition. Sometimes he had had to resort to elaborate scams and cover stories in order to be able to swear that the named person had in fact been served. In past cases Sander had employed various pretexts, including posing as an electric company employee in a uniform he had purchased at a yard sale and as a sweepstakes front man. The latter had been cruel because the target's wife had really believed they were about to share in the Reader's Digest jackpot.

His favorite had been "the auto accident." His client in a divorce case lived out of state and wasn't available to help identify her ex. The matter was complicated by the fact that the ex had a twin. The man lived with his girl friend but, on Sander's first attempt at service, the ex and the girl friend both denied he was the correct twin.

The ex drove an old pick-up with more dents than a golf ball. Sander grew a short scruffy beard to change his appearance, then bought an old junk car with part of the wife's retainer. Next, he staked out the man's truck. When the subject got in the vehicle and pulled onto traffic, Sander maneuvered in front of him. When conditions were right he slammed on his brakes just hard enough to cause a slight rear-ender.

Fearful of a police report and a mark against his insurance, the ex readily agreed to exchange information and settle the matter right there. When the man produced his driver's license, bearing the name and photo of the ex, Sander served him with the divorce papers.

Other times things can get hairy. Private investigators usually only get the summons or subpoenas when the Sheriff's office can't locate the person. Working alone and without any form of radio backup, finding losers who don't want to be found can lead to dangerous conditions. Sander was never without at least one handgun.

At the county road the detective fired up his Harley and rode on back the hollar while his mind worked at trying to come up with a new pretext or a different twist to an old one. About a quarter mile away, a middle-aged woman in overalls was tending a large vegetable garden in front of a neat, clean frame house. He stopped at her gravel drive and, while fighting the chipped stone to secure his kick-stand, the lady approached. "May I help you?"

"Yes, thank you. I'm looking for Billy Cusper. Do you know where I can find him?"

"Why, yes. That's him on that tractor over there," she said, pointing to the field he had just come out of.

Sometimes ya get lucky. By the time he'd turned the heavy bike around on the narrow one lane road, cruised back to the rusty mailbox and secured the kick-stand once again, Cusper was standing next to the pick-up. Leaving his bike running, Sander, subpoena concealed in his left hand, strode right at the 250 pound tractor operator/biker.

"Did you find him, man? I tell ya he won't be back 'till much later. I'll tell him . . . ."

In mid sentence, Sander, now within striking distance, stuffed the court order in the man's shirt pocket, spitting out, "You're Knueson and you've been served, Bobby!"

The roundhouse blow was easy to duck because, like any good cop or P.I., he was ready for it. Now all he wanted to do was get out of there with the minimum amount of damage. Mr. Knueson/Cusper had different ideas. Most perpetrators, once you've beaten them by either placing them under arrest or serving them with process, would curse and yell, call you a few choice names and sometimes take a half-poke at you just to show that they went down swinging like a real man. The guys who don't say anything are the perps you have to look out for. Knueson was silent.

Recovering from the missed punch, Bobby stepped back then forward, cocking his right arm just as Sander buried his fist in the big man's gut. The blow was followed by a pirouette and a side-leg kick to the knee. It was all one movement, but the kick missed, only striking the dirtbag's upper leg. However, the force of the impact did slam

Knueson against the truck. Without a moment's hesitation, Bobby grabbed an iron bar from the bed of the pick-up and raised it above his head as he again advanced.

"Look man, I don't want no trouble. I'm just doin' my job," Sander growled, as he backed away and into a scrub tree he hadn't noticed before. The action shifted into slow motion, a pseudo time deception phenomena known as tachyinterval. Frustration is rampant under this unique condition when events appear to occur in slow motion because the brain is processing more information than the body can react to in a timely manner. He knew the iron bar was coming, knew he couldn't back away in time, knew he had to get his gun out and that the man meant to kill him. But he couldn't understand why it was taking so long to extract the 2 ½ inch barreled Diamondback from his hip holster. Both combatants knew, tachyinterval or not, that once the gun cleared the scabbard and came into battery it was going to explode with flesh tearing, lethal results. Like most important events in life, timing is everything.

At the instant before the revolver, stuffed full of Hornady 125 grain hollow points, reached the point-shoulder position, the thug let the bar fall. The look in Knueson's eyes signaled only temporary surrender as his vengeful stare locked on the vent-ribbed blued steel instrument of death still pointed at him. Slowly they backed away from each other, he toward the double-wide where the rifle and ammunition lay ready on a couch, Sander toward the still idling bike.

Thankful that he had left the bike running while fearful of stalling the engine with a nerve tingling clutch hand, Sander turned and ran for his Harley.

Chapter 10
REPORT TO THE CLIENT

"Hi, it's your favorite private investigator. Got a few minutes?" Sander said into the phone.

"How do you know who my favorite P.I. is?"

"Well, I'd say that whichever P.I. has good news for you would be your favorite. At least until you pick his brain clean and discard him," Sander said. She sure was easy to talk to.

"Okay, so what's the news? Did you find him?"

"Not so fast. If I'm in risk of being discarded after the brain picking, then I want to drag this out as long as I can. After all, it isn't everyday that I get the chance to talk to such a lovely lady."

"Flattery will get you everywhere, Mr. Rackman. Keep talking."

"Okay, how 'bout dinner. After this afternoon I need a big steak, a bigger stiff drink and lots of TLC. If it pleases the court, counselor, the Palm Court at, shall we say, sixish?"

"Perfect. I just have to finish this brief and . . . and I'm looking forward to, ah, hearing about the Knueson matter and . . . ."

"And?"

"And maybe some more flattery."

Swell. Dinner at the Omni with this hunk of a guy and I'm dressed for court. Maybe that necklace in the vault will spice this suit up a little the lady lawyer thought as she twirled the dial to her small wall safe. The vault, discretely hidden behind the Degas lithograph of "Two Dancers at the Practice Bar," was a perk she had insisted on before coming aboard one of Cincinnati's most prestigious law firms. Like many girls who grew up before women's lib, she had always yearned to be a ballerina. She had the talent, but like so many other things in life the timing was never right. First it had been a lack of funds, then her mother's illness. When her mother passed away, she had to come home right after school to care for her siblings. Then . . . well there were just too many other thens. At least now she could afford tickets to the ballet and the artwork she so dearly enjoyed - wonderful illustrations, drawings and a collection of Degas lithographs. Someday, she would own an original.

In the vault she found her David Yurman choker, an exquisite ribbon of emeralds and yellow gold. It contrasted nicely with her off-white tailored suit. Glancing at the clock, she realized she could either finish the brief that was due in Judge Mestemaker's court before noon tomorrow or she could re-apply her makeup and lint-pick her suit. She didn't like to be late at anything and this judge was a stickler for promptness, but priorities are priorities.

At ten before six, freshly made up, she left her Second National Bank Building office for the short walk to the Omni.

"Should I know the guy you were talking to on your way in? He looks very familiar," Sander said, smiling, as he stood to hold Sherri's chair.

She caught her breath when he stood. Even though he wore a sport coat, his button down oxford shirt was tucked into a pair of Levi's! Hardly common attire for the formal Palm Court. This private detective was not a common man.

"Probably. He's Stan Chesley, noted lawyer, very noted lawyer, big shot democrat and genuine nice guy. He's also married to a federal judge. He's the man who headed up the Beverly Hills fire case, the MGM fire in Las Vegas, the Bhopal disaster and many other majors. They call him the master of disaster. He's also Jewish, and I could go for him in a big way if he wasn't married and he wasn't such a bleeding heart liberal and if . . . ."

"And if we had coffee we could have coffee and donuts, if we had donuts," he said, matching her grin.

"Say, that's pretty good. We now finish each other's sentences. Did you know that I'm Jewish? And is it a problem?"

"Of course I know. What kind of a detective do you think I am. I know everything about you: where you live, what kind of car you drive, your bra size, what your favorite . . . ."

"My bra size? How could . . . are you some kind of pervert?"

"Well, maybe I made up the part about the bra size; just testing to see if you were paying attention and not still drooling over the 'master disaster.'"

"Jealous?" she said fully aware that she was flirting like a school girl and that this guy, this unconventional, bike riding, blue jean wearing - gentleman - was stealing her heart.

With a short laugh and a big grin, Sander looked from the stunning emerald necklace to her matching sparkling, viridescent eyes. "When you're the best there is, there's nothing and nobody to be jealous of."

Holding his intense eye contact, the lady Sherri whispered, "You didn't answer my question. Is my religion a problem?"

Still locked in the soft, romantic gaze, he inched within kissing distance, then impetuously grinned. "Gee, what difference should it make between client and private investigator. Is that what you meant?"

She didn't fluster any easier than he did. "Why, of course. What else could I have meant."

She sipped her Bootles Gin and Tonic as he pulled at a Maker's Mark on the rocks. But they both knew what was really meant and she needed to know.

Sherri Foster was born of working class Protestant parents who thought religion was something you only did on Sunday mornings. All through high school she relentlessly pursued the class leader, a Jewish boy, Jack Stein. Believing strongly in the roots of Christianity - that Christians and Jews were all descended from Abraham, Isaac and Jacob - Sherri converted to Judaism before completing high school. Almost immediately after graduation they married. She worked as a waitress while Jack attended college. The Vietnam War intervened and all too soon, Jack was MIA. Their only child, born while his father was away, was killed by a drunk driver before his sixteenth birthday.

Across the room the piano soothed a Johnny Mathis strain, glasses tinkled, black-tied waiters hushed menus du jour and electrified vibes charged at least two of the patrons.

"May I have this dance?" Sander said, not wanting to break the mood as he stood extending a hand.

They walked to an open area near the piano where he gracefully moved her to the mood of the music. The Omni Hotel was originally a Hilton, back when Hilton was king and grandiose was the order of the day. The Palm Court, like the rest of the historic building, had been restored to its former grandeur, complete with crystal chandelier, art deco wall sconces and, of course, the piano bar.

"Sandy, are you sure this is a dance floor? We're the only ones dancing."

Nobody called him Sandy. But, Ms. Foster was not a nobody. "Look, if we're standing on a floor and we're dancing, then this must be a dance floor. Right?"

"Nothing, absolutely nothing intimidates you, does it? Not even the fact that the Maitre d' is giving us dirty looks."

"Maitre ds' are not allowed to give dirty looks."

"Well, if they could . . . he'd be giving us one."

Moving from cheek to cheek to face to face, Sander began in a dignified manner, "Counselor, this court concurs. You're absolutely correct. I mistook this for a dance floor. I beg your forgiveness. It's not a dance floor." Then in a whisper he continued, "It's a kissing floor." He cocked his head and moved his slightly parted lips to within a millimeter of hers. She squeezed his hand, turned her cheek and pressed it to his lips.

With her lips to his ear she whispered, "My mommy warned me about boys like you."

"Then you can't say you haven't been warned, 'cuz I don't take prisoners."

"Prisoners? Is this war? What does that mean?"

"It means that I don't play games - I play for keeps. And all's fair in love and war."

"Are we at war?"

"Either that or love."

Johnny Mathis became Chopin and they walked slowly, arm in arm, back to their table, where their server was awaiting orders.

Over Filet Mignon, steamed snow peas and baked Idaho's au gratin, the lady tried to put business first. "Before you take too much for granted, big boy, let's talk about Mr. Knueson. Has he been served?"

76

"What's wrong with this picture? First, she gets all goo-goo eyed over another hot-shot lawyer, then all she wants to hear about is some sleeze bag."

"I was not all 'goo-goo' over some lawyer. Besides," she smiled tenderly, "I've got the best there is right next to me. Don't I?"

"Case closed!"

"Now, finally, please. Tell me."

"Okay. He was served and the return has been filed."

"How'd you track him down? Did he give you any trouble?"

"Let's, just say he was a mite reluctant to be served."

"What do you mean? I swear, you're worse than a hostile witness on cross."

Sherri sat spellbound, hardly eating, as this gentleman, this seemingly gentle-man, who could be as tough and rough as a bar full of Ironworkers, related the afternoon's activities. He ended with the question: "Since I almost got myself killed, the least you could do is tell me what this case is all about?"

"That's fair, and especially because we're already into a, ah, relationship . . . professionally speaking, of course."

"Of course. What else?" He met her knowing smile.

"This is a pro bono case. Mr. Cusper, correction, Bobby Knueson , has the attention of the Anti-Defamation League of the B'nai B'rith' in addition to others. Do you know who they are?"

"I've heard of them. They keep track of, and investigate, anti-Semitic incidents."

"Very good. This sleeze bag, as you so endearingly - and accurately, I might add - called him, is believed to be one of the henchmen of a very well connected, very well armed and dangerous anti-Jewish gang. My position now, thanks to you, is to file actions against them and seize their property. We have a judgment against a man who can be identified as Bobby Knueson. This is from a fire-bombing of a St. Louis synagogue a few years ago. We traced him to this area but then lost him because we didn't know he was operating under another name. If we can now prove that Knueson and Cusper are one and the same, we will then be able to attach the property you discovered in Indiana."

Over coffee, softened with Baileys Light Irish Cream, she continued. "Though the U.S. Government, because of its sheer size alone, can withstand many attacks by this current wave of anti-government militias and other fanatical groups, the Jews can't. There are only about twelve million of us in this country and any concerted effort to exterminate, or make us out as scapegoats, has to be taken very seriously. Although we're not a fighting people per se - Israelis aside - we are tenacious and well educated.

A warm wind blew out of the southwest ruffling her hair as they walked to her car. Neither spoke, he digesting the night's conversation, she wondering if she had said too much. The romantic mood seemed broken, though they held hands. She opened the door to the little Miata, tossed her purse inside and turned to him thinking: was this six foot, hunk sun-tanned, or was he just dark complexioned like those of Semitic heritage? "Thanks for a job well done, I'm glad you weren't hurt, the check's in the mail and well, I really enjoy being with you, but . . . ."

He moved close to her, trapping her against the car as she raised her hands to signify that she was not receptive to a kiss. "How 'bout a hug?" He impishly grinned. "It's a city ordinance. After dark and after dinner and dancing you have to hug. I'm not foolin'. I'm a detective and I know these things. You want the hug police to arrest you. Do you want to get thrown in the hug slammer? Besides, kisses are only for people who are in love."

She smiled, lowered her arms and like two high-schoolers, they awkwardly and momentarily embraced.

Cleaning what little makeup she wore from her face, she searched the eyes that stared past the eyes of the face in the bathroom mirror. On a night that she had been feeling feminine and capricious her shoulders sagged as melancholy overwhelmed her. Instead of a lace night gown she put on a pair of heavy cotton pajamas. Still unsure of her emotions, she retrieved the box of old photos.

Carefully she rummaged through the remembrances from a past life of love, good times and . . . pain. She stopped at the eight-by-ten of her "soldier," Staff Sergeant Jack Noe. Oh, so long ago, so many dreams, so much love. So many whys.

She was surprised at how young he looked. A beautiful woman, with tears in her eyes and who was now old enough to be the mother of such a young man, stared back at her from the dressing table mirror. She collapsed cross-legged on her canopied bed with a sigh, "Oh, Jack why didn't you come back? Dear God, I converted for him, for You, why did You have to take him? I loved him so.

"We were so happy Jack. Everything was going to be perfect. I tried to do the best I could with Jason, but not having a father for him to bond with, to teach him . . . I'm not trying to excuse myself . . . he's a wonderful boy.

"You'd be so proud of me, Jack. My collection of art is worth more than I paid for it. Yeah, I know you didn't like Degas, but we could have included some Norman Rockwells too. It would have been such fun with you. I'm scared, Jack. I'm involved in some scary things that maybe I shouldn't be."

The former soldier's wife wiped a lone tear from her cheek, sighed deeply and continued softly talking to a picture, a memory of a dream of what should have been. "That's not really why I wanted to talk to you. Ever since I knew that you weren't coming back, oh God how I cried thinking of you in some prison camp – hurt – hungry . . . tortured. I hope you're okay now.

"Jack, I knew this day would come. There's a man. A man I might be falling for. He's a real gentleman and I know you'd like him. He's tough like you were and polished like I knew you'd become. I'm sorry, Jack. I waited and waited. I busied myself becoming an attorney and raising Jason - I'm so sorry. Maybe I should have married somebody, anybody just so our son would have a father. I don't mean a father, but a step-dad to guide him. No one could have been his father except you. Oh, Jack, I needed you so. Tell me it's okay, Jack, I missed you so. I need someone in my life now. Things are getting too complicated for me. I need love and tenderness . . . and help. Is it okay, Jack?"

The secret to life is the ability to adapt to change.

A quiet warmth settled over the soldier's widow as she drifted into a peaceful sleep. The slightly faded photo, lying face up, stared into the glass eyes of her collection of stuffed animals.

Back in his suburban home over-looking a county wildlife preserve, the man who carried a .38 Diamondback under his jacket thought to himself; I enjoy a ride in the country, successfully complete my mission, have a dinner with a very pretty and interesting lady and get paid for all this? Sure hope she has more work for me.

80

Chapter 11
BOOMERS AND 'BOS

He wasn't sure he heard the first torpedo, but the second got his full attention and that of the locomotive engineer who pulled the throttle full back and yanked the whistle chain. Bartlett, fighting the deceleration, coupled with the coupled cars slamming into each other as the slack between them collapsed, strained to reach the window of the cab.

Number 4, a Santa Fe mixed-freight special east bound out of Needles, California, was highballing in high desert country when the emergency stop signals had gone off. These detonation caps are placed on the track to explode when crushed by the engine's wheels – a warning to immediately halt.

Just before the massive 2-10-2 mountain whaler, hissing a fog bank of steam, ground to a stop aside a red lantern, Bartlett caught a glimpse of horses and riders. Highlighted by the massive headlamp he counted at least five with more movement fading into the deep black woods. As a Pinkerton man he was purposely riding in the cab because the Wells Fargo car was heavy with a gold shipment. Specifically on the lookout for trouble he recognized the robbery routine immediately.

The detective jumped from the off-side onto a steeply banked roadbed, pulling his five-inch barreled Colt from its holster. Fighting for footing in the loose rock and gravel he managed to stay in the steam cloud while scampering back to the opening between the tender and the first car. Before he could see the riders, he heard angry shouting from the old hogger, Tom Fiser – demanding to know who, why and what these men on horseback wanted. The answer came with multiple gun shots and the scream of the fireman –

which was followed by a shotgun blast . . . and silence, save for the hissing and ticking of the 2-10-2.

Knowing that life might be over in a flash of gunpowder and wishing he had grabbed his Winchester before bailing out of the cab, Bartlett vaulted over the coupling between the cars shooting at the first rider he saw. Not waiting to learn of his marksmanship, the Pinkerton man wheeled and fanned at least three shots at other men on horseback now visibly painted by the light reflected from the steam. At least three because there were so many shots being fired he wasn't sure how many were his. But, he was sure one of these muzzle blasts caused his left arm to violently twitch. Bartlett tried to vault back over the coupling, but this left arm gave way and he crashed to the roadbed striking his head on the rail. Luckily his momentum carried him over the bed and down into the tumbleweeds and protection of the night.

An explosion ripped the air and produced a flash that silhouetted the entire train. These guys are good, he thought. They've shot the engineer and fireman fought off my return fire and blew the door off the money car in a very timely and precision manner.   But how much time had elapsed?

Lying on the down slope of the raised roadbed, he knew his first priority was to reload. Even with the now searing pain in his left arm, he managed to eject the spent cartridges and stuff the cylinder with six fresh .32-20 rounds. Normally he only loaded five in the six shot single-action revolver as it wasn't safe to carry with the hammer down on a loaded round, but this was a firefight and not carry conditions.

Wide-eyed and ignoring the wound, he crept up the embankment fully expecting gunfire. Nothing. Dead quiet – even the engine. Had he passed out? Where is everyone – robbers, brakemen, Wells Fargo agents, horses? Staggering to his feet, he sought the safety of the engine and what light it provided hoping to retrieve his rifle. At the cab's ladder, using his good arm, he quietly climbed aboard. His rifle and ammo belt were as he left them, though he quickly realized with a bum arm the rifle would be of little use. The fireman, a boomer who was on his first trip firing for the SF, lay across a pile of coal at such an odd angle it was clear he was dead. Tom, however, appeared to have propped himself up against the firebox, but looked slack jawed. Kneeling down, Bartlett could see the stain of blood on Tom's chest, surely a mortal wound.

He had met the hogman on a previous and uneventful run back in '98, when they were a little younger. They had gotten along well, neither man was married, but both had strong family ties and a formidable sense of fairness. Though Tom, ten years his senior, was pushing 40 back then, they had bonded through discussions of family life and treatment of their fellow man. Their first meeting was one of Bartlett's early cases for the renowned Chicago based private detective agency. A thieving brakeman on Tom's train had been surreptitiously tightening select wheel brakes to cause hot boxes. When the conductor ordered the train onto a siding to investigate, the brakeman would slip into a loaded box car and throw out crates of freight to be picked up later by his gang. Bartlett suspected the rouse and was able to catch the crook in the act. That was the easy part. More difficult was tying the yard dicks into the act. The two railroad policemen had claimed they investigated the freight loss but couldn't explain it or catch the culprits. Bartlett, using various methods of, shall we say, persuasion, convinced the brakeman to tell how the S.F. cops were in on the thefts.

Not seeing any sign of the robbers from the vantage point of the cab windows, Bartlett untied the bandana from around the engineer's neck and wiped his friend's face while asking the obvious "how ya doin'" questions. The only response Tom could muster was a pleading look and a beckoning finger. Bartlett leaned close as the old hogger took a breath and whispered, "Will you see to it that my nephew, Thomas, gets my watch and what benefits the S.F. . . . ." He didn't finish as his eyes closed and his fingers relaxed.

No time for bereavement, he had to find the conductor and check the damage and inspect his own wound. Opening the firebox door for light, surprised that the fire was so low, he pulled his shirt off and stared at the bloody upper arm. Using the knife he always carried in his boot, he cut the good sleeve from his shirt and made a bandage as best he could. He was able to move his fingers and the arm, but only with intense pain.

Climbing back down, the first bodies he found were strangers – possibly robbers shot by him due to their proximity to the tender. Hoisting himself aboard the severely damaged W.F. car he found both agents had been blown into the next life by the blast that took the door off their car. The safe had also been dynamited, but Bartlett couldn't remember a second blast – or was this the only blast he heard? These were ruthless men.

"You all right mister?" The voice stunned Bartlett and he dropped, twisted and drew the Single Action Army revolver.

"Don't shoot. We're just bos. Been ridin' in the empty hopper just aft o' this money car," the man dressed as an obvious hobo pleaded.

"How many are you? Where did the robbers go? Where's the conductor and brakemen?" Bartlett demanded, holstering his gun and jumping back to trackside.

84

The bo, terrified and flustered stammered, "You a rail dick?"

"Not likely. I work for Pinkerton. I'm not out to arrest, thump or toss you. Now, where are the others?"

"Back at the end, sir."

By the light of the caboose lanterns, Bartlett came upon an eerie scene that sent a chill through him – the conductor, brakeman and rear brakeman all lay shot dead while some of the hobos were rummaging through the trainmen's pockets. For the third time the detective drew his handgun as he ordered the bos to line up facing the waycar.

Only after asserting they were just trying to get back the four bits each had paid the conductor to ride to Seligman, Bartlett holstered his .32-20. He then discovered there were a total of six men who, hidden in the hopper car, had escaped the slaughter of the robbers. They all had different opinions as to the direction the robbers departed. Additional questioning determined that two of the men were boomers. One, Johnson, a squat looking tough had been a brakeman for the U.P. and the other, Smitherman, a tall gangly kid, was a hostler who had just quit the Needles yard and hopped this special.

"Johnson, you're now the acting rear brakeman. Grab two torpedoes and the red lantern from the dog house and protect the rear of this train. Do you know how to do it?" Bartlett ordered.

"Yeah. I jest go back 'bout a quarter mile an place the bombs on the track 'bout ten paces apart and set the lantern along side."

"Almost right. After you set the torpedoes, you stay there and wave the lantern at any approaching train. Don't come back until you hear our whistle. You got that?"

Turning to assume his task, Johnson mumbled a yes sir.

"Smitherman. Do you think you can move this train if one of these other men fire for you?"

"Yes sir." It was only this here morning that I built the fire in this here very engine and moved her onto the main line."

"Okay, I'm commandeering this train – I'm now the conductor and assume full responsibility. You there," Bartlett said pointing to one of the bos, come with me and Smitherman. You'll fire the engine. The rest of you men load the bodies into what's left of the Wells Fargo car and then you can ride the rest of the way into Seligman in the caboose." Almost as an afterthought, he added, "There's two more in the cab. They were all good men. Treat 'em with respect.

"Once at the station all of you are to stay in the waycar until I say it's okay to leave. That means until after the Marshall in Seligman and I have had a chance to question you. That's an order."

As soon as steam pressure returned to the engine the crippled train and impromptu crew limped the remaining 40 or so miles into the station at Seligman, Arizona.

Bartlett S. Listner (he was never called Bart) had grown up along the Chicago and North Western Railway where his father's life ended in an all too common coupling accident. Pappy Listner, as he was known, was a good father and for as much as Bartlett knew, was a good husband too. Sometimes, though, even good guys die young. For the younger Listner, detective work was also an accident – that of being in the right place at the right time. His father, a C&NW brakeman, had gotten him a job as a call boy for the road. Bartlett's duty was to locate and notify boomers and others on the call board when needed to make a train. He seemed to have a natural ability to find people and the discretion when to not find them plus the physical grit to drag them in when necessary. On a day with a building snow storm he was able to round up, in a most timely manner, the required men to make up a special train. This special just happened to be for a Pinkerton operative who, recognizing Bartlett's abilities, immediately offered him a job.

Arriving at Seligman, the first thing Bartlett did, even before tending to his wounds and reporting to the Trainmaster, was to telegraph Pinkerton headquarters with a preliminary report. Finally, after all reports had been filed, the marshal notified and the men interrogated, he stopped by the barber shop to have his injuries tended. The bullet had passed through his upper arm, just chipping the bone. His head wound, which he now saw in a mirror, was ugly, covered in dried blood and would leave a nasty scar.

Hungry and tired, he took a room at the Harvey House Hotel. Here, after a few hours sleep, he cleaned up and settled into a back corner of the restaurant. Peggy, a vermillion haired Harvey Girl, was first to serve him. She remembered Bartlett as not only had their career paths crossed many times over the years, but they were from the same neighborhood. Their mothers had been friends. She was at least ten years older than Bartlett and had been a real looker - maybe even a dance hall girl - sometime in the nineties. Now, however, her figure gone and in a bland, food stained dress, she was just pudgy dumpy. Friendly, kind hearted, good at her job, a mother image for the other girls, but pudgy dumpy.

"Hi honey. Long time no see."

"Hello, Peggy. It's only been a month or so since I was here last. You doin' okay?"

"They keep me plenty busy. What can I getcha?"

87

While waiting for his food, he wrote a short note on the Harvey House postcards to his mother to let her know he was okay. With the release of the boomers and bos from the official investigation he was sure the story made front pages all across the nation and he didn't want her to worry. Sipping coffee after enjoying his steak and eggs, Smitherman the hostler/boomer, entered the room, looked around and when he saw Bartlett, headed straight toward him.

Without so much as a nod from the detective, Smitherman sat down and, in a low voice, revealed, "It really ain't none of my business, but ol' Tom Fiser was a friend o' mine." Looking around as if worried about his backside, he continued, "I seen three men in the Golden Spur Saloon ah woopin' it up. On the bar in front of them was a Well Fargo pouch – you know the kind they ship gold nuggets in."

"How many horses?"

"There were four tied up right in front of the Spur. But, I only seen three men at the bar."

Wow, this is a break. The robbers weren't even smart enough not to head to the train's destination. Seems these criminals had more dollars than sense. Bartlett thanked the man, paid his bill and kissed Peggy on the cheek before heading for the saloon.

Over confidence, not having a plan and being in a hurry can yield catastrophic events. Luck, however, can negate many such blunders. Bartlett's first mistake was of the self-assurance nature. The second was not securing the help of a posse or even the Marshall. He walked into the bar, stood directly behind the three men with the nugget pouch, drew his Colt and said in a commanding voice, "I'm Pinkerton detective Listner. You are all under arrest for robbery and murder. Place your hands on the bar."

The three men complied at once . . . the fourth – the one Bartlett failed to notice and sitting at a rear table placed his hands on a shotgun. The blast wounded two of the three robbers, but good guy Bartlett, who had not formulated a plan or waited for help, caught the mass of the charge. Like his father before him, sometimes even good guys die young.

Chapter 12
DAY WATCH

"Attention all cars, all departments, armed robbery just occurred, The First National Bank, Kemper and Hilborne, Springdale, Ohio, wanted are two male blacks, armed with a silver revolver, last seen on foot east bound from the bank's parking lot. Car 8-3-8 the North West quadrant. Car 4-6-8 the South West quadrant. Car 4-1-7 . . . ." Springdale, a like suburb just north of us, would respond to the scene, while the county dispatcher assigned beat cars from other suburbs and the sheriff's office to take posts in a quadrant surrounding the area of most probable escape.

Swell. On a beautiful summer morning working my first day shift in months and I've got to find a suitable location where unknown robbers in a non-descript vehicle might be headed my way. Waiting for others to clear their calls, I keyed the mic, "Four-six-eight" okay.

I was, for all intents and purposes working alone, the Chief being the only other Woodlawn officer on duty in our small suburban village. Our head LEO, who always worked the day shift, was dressed in a business suit for the usual meetings and other diplomatic stuff Chiefs have to do.

In my marked patrol car and heading north on Route 4 for its junction with Route 747, I looked at every car coming south. The morning traffic was light and I eyeballed a lone car coming at me - with only one occupant, a male black. The driver looked hard at me, then studied his inside mirror as he passed. Humm. Watching the outside mirror, I used my left foot to apply the brakes to see his reaction. A head popped up! Whoa. One dude hiding in the backseat?

Tripping the roof lights, activating the siren, keying the mic, turning the big '72 police packaged Dodge around on a narrow 4-laner without hitting anyone and then going to full throttle can make modern-day multi-taskers seem like the children's game of dodge-ball.

"Four-six-eight, I'm in pursuit, black over tan late model Chevrolet, southbound Route 4 approaching one-twenty-six. Possible vehicle reference earlier armed robbery broadcast."

"All cars stand-by. Four-six-eight in pursuit. 4-6-8 is this vehicle wanted?"

Facing a double line of cars stopped for the light at 126, I watched the black/tan enter a service station at the corner; drive through the lot and onto Route 126 – a violation of law.

"4-6-8 affirmative. Subject vehicle is now eastbound 126 from Route 4."

I was aware of radio traffic of other cars responding, but my full concentration was on tracking – catching the black/tan. I'd lost sight of them and was approaching Wayne Avenue. Hoping Evendale's 4-1-7 would be coming west on 126, I turned south onto Wayne. About four blocks down, as I blew past a residential driveway, I caught sight of the Chevrolet. Slamming on the binders, jamming the scout car in reverse, I searched for a house number - and the robber with the gun!

"Four-six-eight the vehicle is stopped in the 600 block of Wayne. 2-7."

"Two-seven 4-6-8. 4-1-7?

Out of the corner of my eye I saw one subject running away from the Chevy. I pulled in behind the car that was between two houses and facing a wooded area. Fully aware that at least one desperate man could be hiding behind the buildings, the vehicle, or in the woods - waiting to use the silver handgun or whatever else they might be armed with to ambush me. I didn't hesitate. Service revolver in hand, I approached the black over tan get-away car.

Nothing. Nobody. No sound, save the sirens of my backup. I ran to the woods which was only about twenty yards deep but a block or more long in each direction. No sign or sound of anyone on foot. I headed back to the scene to call in on the radio.

With help from the other officers, we did a cursory search of the Chevy finding a shirt and a chrome plated revolver. Within a few more minutes, a patrol car from another neighboring community, Lincoln Heights, notified the dispatcher he was holding a shirtless, male black subject in a residential yard just three houses away. When the LHPD officer returned to the Chevy, I recognized the man in his custody was the driver of the car that passed me on Route 4.

The shirtless dude, who was 17 years old, told us he was visiting a friend on Marion Road when he noticed his parent's car was no longer parked on the street where he left it. Yeah sure. Since the driver had committed traffic offenses and was at the very least a suspect in a felony, I placed him in handcuffs. Then, I advised the dispatcher of the situation and asked for a Springdale unit to bring a witness to the scene.

Within a short while the witness, a teller from the bank, arrived. He I-D'd the suspect as one of the robbers, and the perp was turned over to Springdale police. The kid later ratted out his accomplice, also 17, and both copped pleas and were placed on probation – this being their first felony.

Day shift is usually the plum, but this day I got a full adrenalin dose before noon. Most action happens between nightfall and three A.M. – second or third shift.

In an average year over 150 police officers are killed in the line of duty – some even by punks younger than 17. You never think about it while it happens, but after arresting any felon, especially when guns are involved, the sweat and shakes usually come-on an hour or so after it's all over.

****

On slow days (there were seldom slow nights) we'd pull out the cold case files and try to think of new angles. One theft caught my eye and sparked my imagination. A contractor had collected money from a retired couple and never did the work. The investigation ended when the address of the contractor turned out to be false.

I started checking with other police agencies and sent QWs to Indiana and the Ohio Bureau of Investigation. Seems the contractor was wanted for theft by deception in Indiana and Illinois as well as other communities in Ohio. Though he always used fictitious addresses, he used his real name and SSN, probably because just moving was easier than coming up with a different driver's license and aliases. With a good license, his MO was to rent a vehicle, but give a false address. He usually paid a few months in advance at the signing of the rental contract and then never paid again. The cars were always found abandoned locally, but before it was considered a stolen vehicle. The pattern of his capers appeared to be one of moving to the next state when the heat became intense. On a hunch that the guy's next move would be just across the river into Kentucky, I started phoning car rental companies in Covington and Newport. Bingo. One rental was to the man I was after.

On my next off day, I visited the rental agency and they allowed me to see the rental contract. The name was the same and he had provided a local phone number. Now for a scam of my own.

The manager of Leather Specialty Company, a local manufacturing operation, was a friend of many years and allowed me to use his company parking lot to set up my trap. I call the perp, and told him I needed some construction work done quickly and cheap. When he hesitated, I hinted that the job might not be within building code standards, and this would be cash only – no contracts or anything on paper and we'd pay half up front and the balance at completion. The contractor's greed got the better of him as he agreed to one last Ohio job. He was to meet me on a Sunday morning in LSC's parking lot. In answer to his questions of where I got his name and number, I told him I was only the production manager and was just doing as the owner instructed. On the remote chance that he might call to check, my friend advised the company receptionist to forward to him any calls for a Jim Fielding, a pseudo name I used for undercover operations.

Arresting felons always follows two procedures: gun pointed at the perp and the verbal command not to move. If there is any movement by the subject under these conditions a shot – or two – or three – is almost always necessary. Perps know this rule of the streets, for sure cops know it, citizens licensed to carry concealed are taught it, and the courts have recognized the ultimate need to protect lives. At the instant of the draw-down it's literally a very tense do-or-die moment. Even though this rule of law is so well known, shots are sometimes necessary – usually because the loser is so high on drugs he doesn't comprehend the command or he's just feeling lucky (a la Clint Eastwood's line from the movie, Dirty Harry).

Sunday morning, off-duty and dressed in a sport coat and jeans, I waited in the department's unmarked car in LSC's parking lot. The day shift officer, my back-up, surreptitiously cruised nearby. Right on time the Kentucky rental car pulled in. I opened the door for the perp, but before he could exit, I asked, "Are you Wendell Cross?" Upon his affirmation, I pulled my Smith & Wesson .38 Chief's Special, shoved it in his neck and said those magic words every cop loves to shout, "FREEZE. POLICE OFFICER. DON'T MOVE. YOU'RE UNDER ARREST."

The second to last thing a morally responsible, prudent person wants to do is kill another human being regardless of how reprehensible, villainous or dangerous that person might be. The last thing this morally responsible, prudent person wants to do is be killed by that reprehensible, villainous and dangerous person."

The back-up arrived as this was going down and we had him in the county jail forthwith.

****

It is said that when one is drowning their entire life flashes through their mind. I've never experienced drowning, but I can relate that there is at least one other condition where one might visualize their life's time line.

My partner, John, and I arrived about the same moment to an ambulance run. Due to the EMTs being an all volunteer department, the county dispatcher always sends the beat cars because the life squad will take a minimum of fifteen minutes. The call involved the vicious dog bite of an eight year old girl. Though she had puncture wounds on her throat she seemed to be breathing normally and there was little blood. John stayed with the family to begin the report while the father took me to the basement garage so I could check the dog's license and rabies tags.

The garage door was open to the fenced-in back yard of this modest middle class neighborhood home. The dog, a German Sheppard mix, lying on the cool concrete as we entered, immediately stood. Though his tail wasn't wagging, he didn't exhibit any signs of aggression such as laid-back ears. Using a soothing voice to keep the dog calm,

I approached. It was a hot day and I was wearing thin, summer weight uniform trousers.

Without any warning the Sheppard lunged for me, locking his jaws on the instruments necessary to extend my family's genealogical line. Pain aside, and only for an instant, it seemed like my entire life was flashing before my eyes. My reaction was to hit the dog as hard as I could. I must have struck his eye or some other tender spot as he immediately released his future-alternating hold. Once free, I pulled my .357 magnum service revolver and told the father to get hold of his dog. He seemed terrified and refused to do so. I then told him to get my partner. Now it was just me and the dog. The stand-off lasted only a few seconds as the Sheppard again advanced toward me. I was ready this time and put a 158 grain semi-jacketed, hollow-point into his chest. He turned and loped into the back yard.

John and I found the wounded animal under a bush, ears pinned back and growling. We both put a couple more rounds into him to end this threat and his suffering.

Checking the tags, which had expired, we asked the dispatcher to notify the county board of health to send someone to pick up the dog to be tested for rabies. By this time the life squad had departed with the little girl. In the privacy of the family's bathroom, John and I checked my injuries. Some blood and punctures . . . and pain. Being the day shift, we were able to reach the Chief and he insisted I drive myself to the hospital to cleanse the bites and for an antibiotic shot. The nurses got a giggly kick out of a uniformed officer with is pants around his ankles.

Within the proscribed amount of time, the health department notified me and the little girl's family that the dog was not rabid.

Chapter 13
SECOND TRICK

My favorite work hours were 3-11, the 2nd shift. Not so much because there was more action, but I would usually be home to see my wife before she went to sleep and I could be up many mornings to play with the kids.

Big city police departments have bureaus for robbery, burglary, bunko – just about anything. Beat cops would take the report and then turn the case over to the appropriate task force, Woodlawn only had an authorized strength of fourteen officers – a number that was never reached while I worked there – thus whoever got the call handled the case in its entirety.

******

Late on a fall afternoon, the call came to "see the complainant" at the local lumber company. Ed McMann, manager, was very distraught. He showed me a bounced check for over four thousand dollars! His story was that a man named Harold Roberts had purchased lumber and tools, produced a driver's license for ID, and took the material away in a large straight truck. Before accepting the check McMann called Northside Bank and Trust, the bank on which the check was drawn. The bank manager assured McMann there were sufficient funds in the account to cover the check.

This could be a significant case for one of Woodlawn's bigger employers. One piece of evidence that turned out to be the saving grace was the truck's license plate number had been written on the loading ticket as was company policy.

First I ran a QW, QV and QCH on Roberts and immediately got a hit. The subject had been arrested in Cincinnati for burglary last year. The QV on the truck came up negative, but a records check with the BMV in Columbus showed the truck was registered to Kevin Kowalski with a Cincinnati address. Kowalski had a lengthy CH and there was an active arrest warrant for him for felony theft and RSG-over (receiving stolen goods over $500 value). He also used a number of aliases. His address was not the same as the address listed for the truck.

Next, with the chief's permission to leave the village, I visited the Cincinnati police records section at District One. Here, Detective Sergeant Oversmith advised that both subjects were known to be members of the Henchmen motorcycle gang.

CPD provided me with mug shots of all the gang members and indicated they had been unable to serve the warrant on Kowalski and two other members with outstanding warrants due to unknown addresses.

I showed the photos to McMann at the lumber company and he identified a Steve Jacobs as the person who purchased the material and tools. This was getting interesting. The following morning, while off duty, I visited the Northside Bank where the manager identified a Paul Twilliger, from the mug shots, as the person who opened the checking account in the name of and with the ID of Carl Zumpstein – two days before writing the check to the lumber company. In addition, he recalled the phone call from McMann, but went on to say that within an hour after the phone call Twilliger came in and closed out the account.

What I was now sure of was subject A, using the ID of Subject B and driving a truck registered to subject C purchased the building materials. Subject D, using the ID of subject E opened and closed the bank account. All of the subjects were believed to be members of the Henchmen MC gang.

The case was complex and would require more overtime and expense than a small department usually wanted to expend. If we could recover the lost funds for their resident lumber company that might be all we could hope for. Police departments are not collection agencies, but some citizens are more equal than other citizens. Therefore and rather than seek indictments, I put out a wanted teletype for the truck which was used in the commission of a felony and, besides, was worth more than the stolen goods.

Never steal less than you can successfully hide and comfortably retire on - after you get out of prison.

A week later, I got a call that the truck had been located in the Mohawk area of Cincinnati. I sent a hook to have the vehicle towed to our impounding lot. Then I waited for the owner to contact me. It didn't take long before an Arnold Jacobstein, an attorney known to represent many of the local underworld, called saying he represented Mr. Kowalski and wanted to know how the truck could be recovered.

My conditions were that Mr. Kowalski - with proper ID, including the truck title - would have to claim the vehicle himself but only after I was notified that the lumber company had been reimbursed for the full amount of the bounced check. The attorney put me on hold to confer with his client. They agreed, if I promised not to arrest Mr. Kowalski when he came to pick up his truck. I approved, but wouldn't promise not to arrest him in the future.

The next evening, following instructions I left with McMann, I received a radio message that the lumber company had been paid. An hour later, I received another radio message to meet a subject at the station reference a truck. Though there were two of us working, my partner was two-seven on another detail and I would have to meet the man wanted on felony warrants alone (after 5:00 P.M. the station was locked and unattended as all of our dispatching was done by the county).

Upon arrival at HQ, I noted the description and license plate number of the vehicle Kowalski was driving in my 2-7 radio transmission. There was another man riding shotgun, but he didn't get out. Inside the station, I made Kowalski write out who he was and what aliases he used. I also photographed him and treated him to a can of Coke. Satisfied that his papers for the truck were in order, I handed him the keys and told him to follow me to the impound lot. I watched the shotgun drive the truck out of the lot while Kowalski followed in the car. They turned south on Route Four, I turned north.

Immediately, I got on the radio saying, "Four-six-eight, two-six, copy one."

When the channel was clear, the dispatcher came back, "Two-six, 4-6-8, go."

"4-6-8, advise Wyoming one Kevin Kowalski, driving a late model Ford Fairlane, two-door sedan, red in color, bearing Ohio 1342 Charles David is southbound Route 4. Subject is wanted on numerous felony warrants."

I didn't arrest him, the City of Wyoming got the collar. Two weeks later, I got a call from Detective Sergeant Oversmith who warned me he had received reliable information that the Henchmen motorcycle gang had put out a contract on me.

Though I always tried to conduct my affairs in condition yellow, I really took Lt. Umbaugh's Law to heart. While attending the Norwood, Ohio Police Academy one of my fellow recruits asked the OIC, Lt. Umbaugh, if we should carry a firearm when off-duty. The sage Lieutenant replied:

"One either never carries a gun

 or one always carries,

   but one never sometimes carries."

****

You know it's going to be a busy shift when going 2-6 from a detail the dispatcher comes back with, "2-6, 4-6-8. Copy 3." Though none of the details we handled that shift were significant, we were kept busy enough for our eight hours to miss a dinner break. Checking into the station a little before the 11:00 P.M. end-of-shift, my partner, John, and I agreed to relax by catching the movie, Dirty Harry, at the local drive-in. After being relieved, we stopped by the 7-11 and split the cost of a bottle of Boone's Farm Strawberry Hill.

Gun belts tossed in the back seat of John's Mustang, but still wearing our uniforms, we settled into a mid-row section and began passing the bottle. Not more than a few swigs into the wine and before the credits had rolled, the guy in the two-door hardtop parked next to us climbed out of his car and stood between the vehicles. John and I looked at each other in total disbelief – this dude was using the speaker pole for a urinal. Ah, man!

John got out as I grabbed a gun belt and followed. The look on this jerk's face when he saw two uniformed cops was almost worth the hassle. We cuffed him and made him sit in his own urine while I went to the refreshment stand to call for the duty officer. The punk was hauled away just in time for us to see the now famous scene where Clint Eastwood spits out the lines:

> "I know what you're thinking: 'Did he fire six shots, or only five?' Well, to tell you the truth, in all this excitement, I've kinda lost track myself. But being this is a .44 Magnum, the most powerful handgun in the world, and would blow your head clean off, you've got to ask yourself one question: 'Do I feel lucky? Well do ya, punk?'"

****

Armed robbery calls, alarm drops, officer needs assistance and other such details that tend to get your full attention can be rough, but another call that is not connected to danger, but is seldom good news is the signal 55 – call the dispatcher. Dispatchers control the radio and it is only when they have confidential or complex information that they ask the beat officer to call them by land line.

At the station, I phoned the dispatch private line, "This is 4-6-8, do you have traffic for me?"

"Stand-by 4-6-8."

"4-6-8? This is Paul Henderson. Who's this?"

"Chuck Klein. Is this bad news?"

"Well, it ain't good. We just got a teletype from North Platte, Nebraska P.D. One Lonnie, Carter has been identified as a hit skip death. They want you to make notification to his family at 10163 Grandview. I'm putting the full message on your teletype"

Being the only Woodlawn officer on duty, I requested to have an Evendale or Sharonville unit handle any details in my bailiwick until notification was complete. We exchanged how-ya-doin's and he gave me the phone number of the NPPD.

Grandview is in the lower middle class area; older, small two bedrooms on a slab with maybe a carport. Most were owner occupied, all were black. Police visits are not looked upon with favor. A middle-aged woman in a house dress answered my knock and before I could utter a word, she announced over her shoulder, "It's the Po-lice."

"Mrs. Carter?"

"Yeah."

"Is your son, Lonnie, the one in Nebraska?"

"Now, what's he done. He's a good boy. Why you here?" She demanded.

"May I come in?" She unlatched the screen door; I removed my hat and walked into a dimly lit living room. Two other people were seated on a blanket covered couch. "We received this teletype," I began, holding it out to her, "Your son, Lonnie, has been identified as the victim of a hit-skip auto accident."

"Oh my heavens. Is he okay?" Her hand, at first held out for the teletype, retracted a little. I stepped forward, took her hand in my free hand and just held it.

"I'm sorry, Mrs. Carter. The police in North Platte, where the accident occurred, said he was killed."

"Oh, Lordy. Oh my poor baby. You sure it be my Lonnie?" Slowly, she reached out with her other hand and took the yellow paper.

"I'm not sure of anything, ma'm. There's a phone number on the sheet for you to call."

"We ain't got no phone. How we gonna call all the way out to Ne-braska?"

"If you come to the station you can use our phone. I'm sure the Chief won't mind. You can also call your preacher or any other relative if you'd like. Do you have a way to get to the station?"

> To a parent, nothing, absolutely nothing, can emulate the loss of a child.

She sat in a chair and fanned herself with the teletype as the man and young girl, who had been on the couch, came over to her. I felt like the grim reaper in neon lights. After a few moments and a glass of water brought by the girl, she gathered her strength, "It be all right. Maybe it jest be a mistake. Thank you officer. We be right down to the station."

She was a brave woman with a lot of composure. In the shadows, I couldn't see the tears, but I could hear them in her voice – something I could personally relate to having lost a child myself. Though most recollections of my tragic loss are blocked out of my memory, the part that isn't is the reassuring strength I got from a crisp uniform and calm voice of the responding officer. I straightened up a little more, hoping she got the same from my presence. I replaced my cap, came to attention, and I don't know why, but I saluted before turning to go.

Back in the cruiser and before keying the mic, I heard 4-5-6 being sent to a "see the complainant" in my town. Some things are more important as I advised the dispatcher I was remaining 2-7 to the station.

Chapter 14
MORE, FROM THE OTHER SIDE OF THE BADGE

In the early portion of 1957, I truly awoke. Rock & Roll was in full control, girls were suddenly of interest, and for my fifteenth birthday, my father bought me a car!

The car, a '52 Crosley two door sedan with its tiny four cylinder engine that barely ran, was a real dream to me. The dream being to convert this slow, top heavy, unattractive, little-old-ladies-mobile into a screaming, low slung sports car. To accomplish this would require replacing the metal body with a new, racing style fiberglass shell and hopping up the engine or maybe stuffing a V8-60 between the rails.

The magazine advertisements for the Almquist plastic body declared the average installation time should be fourteen hours. They lied. My father must have known this because what could a fifteen-year-old, sans license, do with a real sports car? Of course, not having a license didn't stop me from putting a few "test" miles on the stocker during post midnight joy rides when all were asleep. Once actual construction began, the car would be totally undriveable - except in the various stages when tests were "required".

By late spring, I had the body off and faced the grinding task of cleaning the remains. The drudgery of this work was mind numbing and the dirt and filth was so heavy that I had to spend a good portion of each day just cleaning the garage. The garage was surrounded by shade trees and the area remained quite cool in the summer as the house was not air-conditioned. On one outside wall, under the wood double hung windows, was the heart of the workshop; a large work bench, some eight feet long. We made this bench from wood my brother, Willie, and I had swiped from some of the new houses under construction in the area. This creation was made of plywood and two-by-fours and held together with nails, since by that stage of life we hadn't discovered threaded fasteners. It was sturdy enough with a full length shelf underneath and was eye-ball level to a floor.

When the fiberglass body arrived from Almquist a quick check of the dimensions showed that there was no way it would fit and look right. There weren't any instructions, just a shell, two curved pieces that had to be fitted and made into doors, and a copy of the invoice showing that the amount of $295.00 had been paid. For the finished car to look and handle correctly, the engine would have to be moved down and back plus "Z'ing" and "C'ing" the frame. Alterations I had only read about in hot rod magazines.

The end of fall found the bodiless roadster ready for a road test. All that was required for this trial were weather conditions of least thirty-plus degrees and dry. Not normal for this time of year, but I had faith that the Gods of high speed would smile on me. Sure enough, I got the bright sun-shiny day only it happened to arrive during school hours. All I could think about the entire morning was the test drive and, by sixth bell, I could resist no longer. I cut Biology and quickly thumbed home.

Exchanging my school outfit for the warmest clothes I could find, I headed for the garage and a date with excitement and apprehension. Without wasting any precious fair weather, I fired up the now souped-up engine which had, in addition to a Harmon-Collins cam, a fifty thousand volt coil and dual point distributor. I listened to the idling four-banger, which was music to my ears, trying to familiarize myself with its every sound for reference after the test run. I had to rig a piece of bailing wire to the throttle linkage on the carburetor because there was no floor board to affix a gas pedal. I sat on a piece of plywood - poised my left foot on the clutch and my right foot as near to the brake pedal as possible and eased the bomb down the driveway.

My plan was to drive to the area of streets across the main road that ran through our small village. On the way over I rolled the car from one side of the road to the other, all the while watching the frame for any signs of stress. The quick steering was perfect, a result of the lengthened pitman arm. It took less than one full turn for lock to lock. At the entrance to my "test track", I doubled clutched into first gear, listened to the engine, took one more look at the frame welds, and grabbed the makeshift throttle. The instant I yanked on the wire the tires spun, and the bodiless car rocketed forward almost causing me to lose my grip on the steering wheel. The force of this sudden acceleration was so great I couldn't lift my foot to depress the clutch, and by the time I had let go of the throttle cable, the car was half on the grass shoulder of the road. Holy cow, I could get really hurt, I thought, as I lined up for another try.

Calming myself, I gripped the wheel with renewed strength, I felt a rush of adrenalin as I dumped the clutch while tugging at the cable. This time I held the little beast in a straight line. I reached about fifty in second gear and noticed the main frame section was bowing out, but the front end was very stable and I pushed on, taking the first turn on rails. It hugged the road like asphalt to a pothole. Now I was sailing down the short, flat straight to the second turn where I applied full power half way through and promptly spun out, narrowly missing a tree. This was like, crazy man! I loved it!

On the back straight, now in third and at a higher speed, I could clearly see the frame bowing out. Time to take it home, one run was enough for now. Once inside the garage, I could hardly push the clutch in because I was shaking so much.

In late January, using large pieces of corrugated cardboard from my father's factory, I made a floor board template. A local sheet metal shop then fabricated the floor board. With the help of a few buddies, the body was placed on the now completed chassis. I used fiberglass cloth over wire mesh to make "L" brackets which were then bolted to the floor board/frame and glassed to the body.

The first day of spring came and went without any fanfare. I was almost sixteen, and my car was done except for the paint. I decided to take one final shakedown run before painting in case any major changes were required. Friday after school, weather permitting, would be the first day for a test with the body on, license or no license. After a brief warm up and a check of the recently installed Stewart-Warner gauges, I headed for my test track. Now, with a seat to hold me and an accelerator pedal I could really see how it would handle. This time when I dumped the clutch, I easily kept control as the little bomb shot down the straight-a-way. At turn number one I doubled-clutched down into second and pushed the car through on rails not ready to try a full drift. Turn two was the same though I took up the entire width of the road. Accelerating into the back straight, the muffler-less exhaust produced an ear splitting pitch as the little four banger turned upwards of eight-thousand RPM.

The thought of disturbing any of the people living on this normally quiet street never occurred to me - at least not on the first trip around. The only negative observation I had was that the engine seemed to flatten out well before it should. Maybe the stock carb was not enough for the hot cam. At the end of the first run, I was enjoying it so much that I decided to go again, this time trying for a little more speed in the corners.

Heading into turn one, I tried what I had only read about; the four-wheel drift. Just before the apex and at about thirty miles per hour I jerked the wheel hard left, which, as it should, started the front end sliding. At this attitude, if I did nothing else the car would plow off the road. If I backed off the gas, I would spin out. However, I forced myself to do what I had read about; I opened the throttle full sending the little sports car into an actual four wheel drift - if only for a second. I over-corrected and did a complete one-eighty right in the middle of the street. It was exhilarating. Here I was doing what I had only dreamed about doing and doing it with a car I had made. I got straightened out and headed for turn two where I was determined to master the drift.

This time I got it right. However, unknown to me, old lady Fritz, who lived just past turn two, had had time to get her broom ready when she heard me start my second trip around. Now, here I was coming out of a controlled slide with no place to go other than into a tree or right past the edge of her drive where she stood, broom in hand. She was either crazy or had more faith in my driving than I had because the line I was taking was going to put me within inches of where she stood. She didn't budge and as I got within swinging distance, she gave the broom a round house swipe at me, knocking the tiny Plexiglas windscreen loose from its retaining bolts. I ducked and didn't get hit, but I could hear her screaming something as I slammed into third gear. Enough! Get me back to the garage.

I hadn't been home long enough for the engine to cool down when the police pulled up. I approached the open window of the scout car just as Officer Bloomfield was saying into the mic, "Twenty-one, two-seven the Klein residence."

"Two-seven, Twenty-one. Advise the subject if I catch him racing that thing, he's going straight to Juvenile," came the voice over the radio.

Uh oh, I was in big trouble now. I could just see my chance of ever getting a license fly right out the window.

"Chuck? It's Chuck, isn't it?" The uniformed cop asked.

"Yes sir."

"Maybe I better take a look at this thing you've been terrorizing the neighborhood with. Is that it?" He said, nodding toward the garage.

I stood over to one side as he walked around my pride and joy which was squeezed between parts boxes and the work bench - the one made from stolen lumber. Maybe they were still looking for the thief, I thought; sweat beginning to form on my forehead. He didn't say anything for the longest time, just peering into everything. Finally, the officer reached back to where his handcuffs were. I looked out the door at the woods. I could run and hide in one of the old tree houses, and when it got dark, I could thumb to Texas or someplace, anyplace. Thoughts of prison raced through my mind as he casually hitched his up his pants and said, "Did you build this yourself?"

"Yes sir," I replied with a voice that resonated with guilt.

"Pretty good. I wish I'd had been able to do something like this when I was younger. You've got quite a place here, with that work bench and all."

He did know! Now the axe is going to fall. If I made a break for it, he might shoot me. I had visions of my body lying spread eagle on the driveway. I wondered if the bullet in my back would hurt more than the falling on the blacktop. I suddenly had an over-powering urge to fess up, but my throat was all choked and I couldn't speak

"Can I take a look at the engine?" Officer Bloomfield asked, without commenting on my total silence. He reached for the leather straps that held the hood down while I hurried to assist, still unable to talk. Maybe the parts I got off old man Crifield were stolen, This is crazy. I've got to get

110

hold of myself and start acting cool. I grabbed the straps on my side of the car and helped the officer lift the hood.

"Looks like you've done a lot of work on this, fellah," the cop commented, admiringly. Silence. "I'll tell you one thing, Chuck. You're pretty cool. There's no question that this engine has recently been run, I can feel the heat from here, and there's no doubt in my mind that this is the car Mrs. Fritz described as almost running her down. However, since I didn't see you driving it and you have had the presence of mind not to admit to anything, there's nothing I can do other than let you know that if we catch you, it'll be a citation at the least. And if Sergeant Prince catches you, well, you heard him on the radio; he'll haul your sorry tail to Juvenile Hall. Is that clear, son?"

I couldn't believe my ears. "Yes, sir," I said, in as normal a voice as I could muster.

"I'm not going to give you a ticket or even tell Prince, but I would like to know, just for the sake of truth: How fast were you going around that corner at Mrs. Fritz's? She said you were going at least fifty, but I don't think any car could go that fast around that narrow corner."

"You mean no matter what I say, I won't get into trouble?" I asked, still not believing my good fate.

"That's right. Off the record."

"Well, I don't really know as the rod doesn't have a speedometer, but I'm sure I was going at least forty, sir."

"You can cut that 'sir' bit too. I'm Tony and the official investigation is over. I'm impressed. Your car looks like it should be something you can be proud of, and from what you tell me and what Mrs. Fritz said, it must handle better than anything I've seen."

"Thank you. Do you want me to fire it up so you can hear it?" I offered, but still afraid to call him by his first name.

"Maybe some other time. I better get back on the air or the Sarge will come looking for me himself." I followed him to the cruiser and listened as he called in.

"Twenty-one, two-six."

"Two-six, Twenty-one. Were you able to catch the little whippersnapper?"

"Negative. Subject vehicle was in garage, and I was unable to determine who the driver was." Tony hung the mic back on the dash and said, "Look Chuck, you better take it easy here in the Village. Even a dog knows not to dump where he eats, if you know what I mean."

"You're right, Tony, I'm sorry. I'll try to keep my testing to the strip."

As the cruiser drove away, a wave of exhaustion swept over me. My emotions had been on a wild roller coaster, and I was too whipped to think about anything, even the flatness of the engine at high speed. I went inside only to face an inquisition by my mother.

****

Late on a summer night, I noticed my buddy Howard's '57 Chevy in the lot at the White Castle drive-in. Pulling up next to him, I said, "Hey man, I see you finally got that junker runnin'."

"This "junker" will dust you off any time you're ready," came the reply from Hard (as he was known, 'cuz that's how the Kentuckians he worked with pronounced Howard).

Before I could think of a good come-back, Louie Wolpa walked over saying, "It's about time you two smoked one off." Howard and I looked at each other and grinned.

"I'm ready, if you are," he said.

"Wait a minute. What have you got in this thing? You're too eager. Pop the hood and let me see," I demanded.

"Fine with me. It's just a stock two-seventy."

"Bull! You never drove a stocker in your life."

He opened the hood, but all that was obvious were two-four's. Anything else had to be hidden in the engine. "Fire it up one time, Hard," I insisted.

When the engine caught I could tell by the sound that it had a hot cam, maybe an Isky 5-cycle? "How big did you bore it and what's the cam?" I said, probing for information.

"Now look, do you want to talk or do you want to race?" Howard took a hard line and I knew it was now or never.

"Okay. But no standing start. We go from a roll. I'll take Louie and you get a passenger to count."

The rules were made and we pulled onto north bound Reading Road. Leveling off, side by side between twenty-five and thirty, I rolled my window down to hear the count. Howard's passenger shouted above the din, "One . . . two . . . three!"

I didn't drive a stocker either, as I had installed a Clay-Smith full race cam and a few other goodies on my bored and stroked '49 Ford flathead. At the sound of the magic number, I stabbed the throttle opening all six of my two-barreled carburetors. The sudden acceleration of this ten year old sedan slammed me back in the seat. I fixed one eye on the tach and put my full attention into hearing the engine. I got the jump on him; the recent tune up had not been in vain.

In second gear my lead increased, but once into third and as we neared the top of the hill, just before Langdon Farm Road, he began to close the distance - his two-four's and whatever else he had, now had the edge.

Cresting the hill, abreast of each other and at a little over a hundred, our headlights picked up the reflective decals of a city police car waiting for the light at Langdon Farm. It was too late now. I could see by the condition of the "walk-wait" signal that the light was not going to remain green for our north bound cars. We went through the red light together at something over fifty, hands on horns, high beams bright and engines revved tight. The cop didn't waste any time in turning on his bubble gum machine and pulling out around the line of cars waiting with him. Howard stopped in front of the high school, but I kept right on going into the suburbs. I wasn't worried about a road block because the city and the villages were on different radio frequencies. The last time I saw the cop, he was about a half-mile back and losing ground.

Once at home, I put the Ford in the garage and found a key to my sister's car, which we took back to White Castle. Hard was waiting for us, grinning from ear to ear. He explained how John-law pulled next to him, told him to wait, and took off after me. As soon as the cop was out of sight, Howard merely turned around and drove back to the drive-in. The cop, obviously a rookie, had failed to copy license plate numbers or even get a good look at Howard and we were now both scot free.

****

Just after my 18th birthday, my buddy Howard and I decided to take our spring vacation in Florida. We made two mistakes. One was telling friends our plans and two, was using my father's car.

Arriving in St. Petersburg on a warm, sunny Friday, we flopped the top of the new 1960 Corvette and within minutes had two pretty sisters showing us the way to the beach. By Saturday night both of us had found jobs parking cars at an area night club. We had slept the first night on the beach and then spent the days sleeping at the girls home while their parents were at work.

At the end of the first week of this dream life, and three days beyond our school's spring break, the police pulled us over. They didn't ask any questions, just arrested us for driving a stolen vehicle. Seems my father was a mite upset that I had taken the car he had bought and paid for, skipped school and took off without even saying goodbye to my mother. Howard's mom and dad were also behind this strategy to have us slammed in the slammer.

The jail cell was packed with six bunk beds, a toilet and wash stand; and though it was broom clean the prisoners weren't. This was not a Mr. Bojangles kind of place. My five fellow inmates were unshaven, scruffy, smelly and mean looking. The jailers took my wallet, money and car keys, but allowed me to keep my cigarettes and lighter. I sat on an empty bed, and thinking that I was tough and cool, lit a Pall Mall.

Finishing the fag, I causally strode to the toilet and deposited the butt. WHAM! I was grabbed from behind, spun around and slammed into the wall by a foul breathed, tattooed heathen who threatened, "You best pass be passin' on your butts, boy. We don't throw 'em away here."

"Yeah, sure. I'm, I'm sorry. I didn't know. You can have the whole pack."

"Naw. You keep 'em. Jest don't be throwin' away no butts."

Next time I had the urge for a smoke; I took two drags and immediately handed it to the guy sitting across from me. By morning, after a sleepless night, I was ready to promise anything to get out of there. The police and our parents had conferred, allowing us to motor slowly back north, re-enroll in school and to stay out of trouble.

Chapter 15
GRAVEYARD SHIFT

Of the three shifts, the third, eleven to seven or midnight to eight, is the best as far as working conditions go. After the drunks have made it home, to jail or some other immovable object, things quiet down to the point where any radio traffic is usually something heavy. Other benefits include having no problem staying up late to party on off days - and acute night vision. The squad car's dash lights are kept in the dimmest setting and sun glasses are the requisite for code 7 breaks. It takes about a week of working the third to really appreciate and recognize the pronounced increase in the ability to see in the dark.

If you've ever noticed how much better you can see at night after your eyes adjust – multiply that intensification by ten and you get the idea of how significantly your vision increases when your eyes have had the opportunity to improve over many strung together third shifts.

On a cold winter night, just past two in the morning, it was our turn to be the center of a quadrant. Breaking squelch on the so-far quiet night the county dispatch intoned: "Attention all cars all departments armed robbery just occurred the Kay-O station State Route 126 and Wayne Avenue Woodlawn Ohio. Wanted are two male blacks last seen east bound 126 from Wayne in an older model Ford sedan, green in color." As the quadrant was being set up, I headed to the Kay-O gas station while John radioed he would be east bound on 126.

At the gas station the lone attendant, Wilber Johnston, as expected, seemed nervous. When I began to question him about what happened he became agitated saying he had already given that information to the dispatcher. I explained that the dispatcher was not a Woodlawn police officer and I

117

needed first-hand details for our report. He relented, nervously telling me after gassing up a 1961 or 1963 blue Ford the driver pulled a small revolver and demanded all the station's money. Johnston continued on saying he was the only attendant working and carried the station's cash on him. He estimated the robbers got about $300.00.

Something didn't quite click and it took a few seconds for it to register. I asked Johnston to produce his identification – for the report – and requested he again describe the vehicle. His social security number was issued in Florida, but he had an Ohio driver's license with a local address. Giving me a look of, I already told you, he reiterated the vehicle was an older Ford sedan, he wasn't sure of the year, and it was blue in color.

I thanked him for his patience and told him to call the station owner while I worked on the report. While he was inside the station, I requested permission from the dispatcher to contact him on channel two. Police channel two on the county band was reserved strictly for police to police confidential communication. The news agencies were not supposed to monitor this channel.

Permission granted, I asked what the complainant told them as to the color of the robbery vehicle. The dispatcher who took the call immediately played the recording tape back and advised the robber's car was described as green in color. After I told him of my conversation we agree to cancel the quadrant and issue a code 4.

Within a few minutes John arrived at the Kay-O station, all questions. We conferred and agreed that it would be best if we took Johnson in for further investigation. By this time the Kay-O station owner had pulled in and we related our suspicions to him.

On the pretext that another agency might have captured the robbers and we would need him to identify them,

Johnston was brought to the police station. Once at our HQ, John and I began a Mutt & Jeff routine. Since I had already established myself as the good cop, John lit into the now suspect threatening to beat the stuffing out of him if he didn't confess. I tried to look helpless and walked out of the squad room. While John continued his interrogation, I called dispatch and asked them to run a QW and QCH on the man.

Time for the good cop to return. Seeing the suspect wide-eyed and drained of color, I said, "Why don't you let me talk to him for a few minutes Patrolman Campbell? Perhaps Mr. Johnston would rather talk to me." John knew the routine and, after a hard glaring stare, stalked out of the squad room.

Tossing my pack of Lucky's on the table for him, I said in a calm understanding way, "We know you weren't robbed, It will go a lot easier on you if you come clean and tell me what really happened." I watched him relax a little as he lit one of my cigarettes. "Did you work this alone or have a partner?" Still no response. "Okay, but if you don't tell me, I'll have to turn you over to Patrolman Campbell and I won't be able to help or protect you from him." I could see the consequences banging around in his head as I turned to walk out of the room.

"Wait, wait. I'll tell you. There wasn't anyone else. I put the money in my car and told the dispatcher guy I was robbed. How did you know?"

Before I could answer his honest question, John returned, backed me out of the way and drew his service revolver saying, "Don't move Johnston. You're under arrest for armed robbery and murder!" Now it was my turn to be all questions. Though John had patted Johnston down before placing him in his patrol car, we gave him a thorough search before placing him in the holding cell. It was then that John handed me the teletype. The QW came back as a signal 30.

Johnston was wanted on armed robbery and murder warrants in Florida.

While John worked on his report, I called the dispatcher to thank him and let him know we had things under control and to notify the Florida agency holding the warrants we had their man. Next I visited the cell and asked the felon if he would sign a consent to search his car. At first he refused, then relented when I hinted John would be back to make the same request.

We found the money, filed misdemeanor charges of making a false report to police and placed him in the county jail to await Florida's pleasure.

****

Uniformed police officers have virtual absolute power at all emergency locations except one: the fire scene. Here, the fire chief's word is supreme. He has the right and the power to command any and all persons at the scene of a fire, including police officers.

It was mid-watch, around 3:00 a.m., and I had just pulled into an all-night restaurant in Sharonville, hungry for a plate of bacon and eggs over easy with english muffin and lots of fresh black coffee. Leaving the beat for a meal break is permitted so long as it's close, things are quiet and there's another officer on duty to cover the details. Sometimes we eat in Sharonville; sometimes Sharonville cops eat in our town.

"4-6-8, code 7."

The radio was quite and had been so for some time. After a minute of silence, I tweaked the squelch knob thinking maybe the radio was not working – or maybe the dispatchers were code 7 too. I waited a minute or so and again said, "4-6-8, code 7."

This time the radio talked back, "Stand-by 4-6-8."

Uh oh. This isn't good. I put the scout car in gear and began heading back to our village. Within a minute the radio came alive again. "Attention, cars 4-6-8, 4-7-0, 4-1-7, 4-1-8 dispatching your fire companies to 359 Holmes Avenue, Lincoln Heights, the Rest-Easy nursing home. Car 4-6-8 . . . ."

As primary beat car, I headed for the fire location – it just seemed like the right thing to do. The Lincoln Heights Fire Department was already fighting the blazing single story building and had put out the call for help as soon as they arrived. I checked in with the Chief who told me to block the west end of Holmes to keep people out and cars off the fire hoses.

Even from a block away, it was obvious the building was going to be consumed. I didn't know if anyone was inside or if there were any injuries, but three life squads soon arrived. With enough equipment and the fast call for help, the fire was out by six-thirty. The fire chief sought me out and told me to follow him as he related the possibility of arson and that the fire scene must be preserved until an investigation was complete.

The chief led me to a basement door saying, "Stay here, officer, and do not allow anyone into the basement. No one except me or the state fire marshall when he arrives. Is that clear, officer?"

"Yes, sir. Very clear."

My shift ended at seven, but I couldn't leave this post until relieved – and I was really hungry. Though Red Cross had arrived while the fire was still active and had brought me and others hot coffee and donuts, I still craved a plate of bacon and eggs.

Just after seven, four men, dressed in suits, approached my post. As they started toward the basement door, I shifted my position saying, "I'm sorry, gentlemen, the fire chief as instructed me not to let anyone into the basement."

"I'm the Mayor here and I want to see what's down there," one of the men officially demanded. I reiterated my position feeling very nervous that here I was, a Woodlawn officer, telling the Mayor of Lincoln Heights – in Lincoln Heights – what he could not do.

He was in my face now, spouting threats of "I'll have your job, patrolman. Get out of the way." I stood my ground saying, if he tried to pass me or touched me, I was going to physically arrest him. I also told him to take up his demands with the fire chief. The crisis passed.

Twelve elderly patients died in the fire, most in their beds. The Governor of Ohio visited the scene later that day and vowed to seek better fire protection for nursing homes. It was determined to have been arson, but no indictments were ever handed down.

Police officers appear jaded and uncaring, because they are exposed to tragedy, unspeakable crimes, victims of abuse, and other horrors. This is not the case. Deaths and dreadfulness leave their mark and sometimes the only way cops deal with it is to make light of it – among themselves - or escape into the bottle. That morning, as soon as I was relieved by a Lincoln Heights officer and the fire chief, I headed for some bacon and eggs – not because I was hungry, but so I didn't have to think about flames terrifying and overwhelming the helpless, bed-ridden seniors.

****

"Whats you mean, I be under arrest. I was the one shot! How come you not be arrestin' the shooter!!?" The ex-con, Jerome Damond, demanded as Sergeant Thacker and I cuffed the dude in the hallway of the county court house. We had all come out of the Prosecutor's office adjacent to the Grand Jury room where evidence was presented that Lawrence Nathan admitted to shooting Damond. But, Nathan was not arrested – Damond was.

This incident grew out of an altercation at the Country Kitchen restaurant about a month previous. Damond, was causing a disturbance and refused to leave the eatery. Nathan, the manager, got a tiny .25 ACP pistol from his office and, without pointing it at Damond, ordered him out. Nathan claimed, and no witness disputed this, Damond with fists clenched, advanced toward him in a menacing manner. It was then that Nathan shot him. The problem was, the bullet hit Damond in the buttocks.

The Sergeant and I, and all the cops in the area, knew and liked Nathan. When we were called to the scene, we ordered a life squad for Damond and conducted an interview of those present – including manager Larry Nathan. Back at the station, I completed the incident report and presented it to Sergeant Thacker for his approval. Because it was close to the end of our third shift, we waited for the Chief to arrive – after all this did involve a shooting.

The Chief didn't like the way it was handled, indicating that we should have arrested Nathan and turned the case over to the prosecutor to take before a Grand Jury. The Sergeant and I drove back to the Country Kitchen and, as apologetic as we could be, took Nathan to HQ to be printed and photographed.

In the Grand Jury room, based on our testimony, we were able to convince the jury Nathan fired in self defense, and at that instant, Damond turned away thus causing the bullet to strike him in the rear. No one wanted to see the nice guy restaurant manager convicted of any crime. Nor did we want to allow a dirtbag such as Damond to issue threats with impunity. After the proceedings, the Sergeant and I discussed the issue with the prosecutor who agreed that the Grand Jury testimony gave us probable cause to arrest Damond for assault. There is no statute, law or constitutional right that guarantees that life is fair.

As we led the ex-con to the county lockup, he looked at me saying, "I'll getcha, pig. Some night you be drivin' that fancy po-lice car down the road and I'll be shootin' you like Larry shoot me." I spun him around and slammed him against the wall, "Listen punk you might be able to ambush me, but try to keep this in mind; ninety-six percent of all cop killers are caught. Of that 96%, after and if they get out of the hospital, 100 % go to the chair. And while you're waiting for that jolt of juice the guards will give you special treatment – if you dig what I mean. You think you're not being handled fairly now, just try offing a cop, scum."

****

Another loser who found out that life isn't always fair was the biker who, according to him, ran out of gas at a closed gas station. It was deep into my third when I just caught the outline of a Harley parked next to the gas pumps at the closed Sohio station on Wooster Pike in Terrace Park. Working alone and not knowing what I had, I asked for a Milford unit to meet me there. By the time I got turned around and stopped at the entrance, to run my spotlight over the building, the biker came out from behind the pumps to stand next to his hog. He was wearing the colors of the Outlaw Motorcycle club. Mindful of the contract that had been put out on me by the Henchmen MC gang, I realized this guy could be acting for the Henchmen, casing the station for a burglary or . . . .

Keeping him in the lights of the cruiser, I got out and approached from a right angle asking what the problem was. The biker said he was out of gas and had used the pay

124

phone outside the station to call a friend who was bringing him some fuel.

About this time Patrolman Ocker with Milford P.D. arrived. We had the biker produce his license and registration for the dispatcher to run through NCIC. The computers were down which called for a diversion. While Ocker kept the gang member busy with questions, I pulled out of my squad pack a baggie partially filled with pipe tobacco. Concealing the bag in the palm of my hand, I approached the Harley and looked down, saying, "What do we have here?" I then produced the bag making it appear that I had found it under the seat of the hog. The biker knew he was in trouble stammering that the bag wasn't from his bike and he wasn't causing any trouble. I looked at Ocker and said, "Officer Ocker, did you see me take this bag from under the seat of this motorcycle?"

"Yes sir I did."

"I'll bet if we have the lab test its contents it will turn out to be full of Mary Jane." I then turned to the one with the Outlaw colors and said, "There's no question in your mind that the bag will turn out to be marijuana and we'll have a warrant for your arrest, is there?"

He looked at his boots. "No sir."

"I'm not a mean sort of guy, so I'll tell you what I'm going to do. I'm going to hold this bag for evidence, but not seek a warrant provided I don't' catch you in my town again."

Ocker and I went back to our respective patrols and the next time I passed the Sohio station, the bike and biker were gone.

Chapter 16
FUN & FUNNY DETAILS

It was a little past two a.m. and patrolman Terry Bennett, the only officer on duty in the small Cincinnati Suburb of Terrace Park, had just opened a fresh cup of coffee. Parked in plain sight on U.S. 50 and facing Indiana Hill Road, he watched the digital radar screen climbing as a car approached. Ah man, he thought, I don't care how fast you go; just don't blow off the stop light, I want to enjoy my coffee.

The radar indicated the approaching car was passing 60 MPH in this narrow, tree-lined residential, 25 mile zone.

Surely he can see me and wouldn't dare run the light. Damn! He did.

Tossing the fresh cup out the open window, Terry tripped the roof light, jammed the shift lever into drive and mashed the throttle to the floor while grabbing the mic. The sudden and rapid acceleration of the Highway Patrol packaged cruiser slammed Bennett into the seatback as he said, "Four-six-one I'm in pursuit." Because there were over three dozen agencies on the single county radio band, protocol, even for an emergency, was to make as brief a call as necessary for fear of walking-on (talking over) another officer who might have a greater need.

The dispatcher came back immediately, "All cars stand by. 4-6-1 in pursuit. 4-6-1 4-4?"

"4-6-1 inbound Wooster in pursuit late model Chevelle black in color. Subject vehicle exceeding 75."

Wooster Pike, the main thoroughfare through Bennett's bailiwick was officially U.S. route 50 and aka, Wooster, Bloody Wooster, due to its narrow four lanes. U.S. 50 ran from coast to coast, but only 2.4 miles of it were in Terrace

Park, Ohio. West of the bedroom community's corporation limit (inbound as in toward the city), it became county jurisdiction. Because of mutual aid agreements between all the Hamilton county police agencies chasing violators in hot pursuit was permitted and protected.

About four miles from the jurisdiction line was the first intersection, Church Street, where a Sheriff's Deputy and scout cars from the adjoining villages of Newtown and Mariemont would be converging in hope of setting up a road block.

As Bennett entered the sparsely populated unincorporated zone, he activated the siren, though the Chevelle was at least a mile ahead. Keying the mic again he tried to keep his voice calm, "461 I'm running 85 and can't catch him."

"Okay, 4-6-1. 4-0-8, 4-3-6, 9-1-2 are you aware of 4-6-1's traffic?"

Each, in turn, acknowledged the dispatcher and indicated their destination was the intersection of Church and Wooster for a road block.

Rounding the bend just before the Church Street intersection, Bennett could see the line of police cars with their red lights flashing. He could also see the Chevelle dead stopped and hard into the curb.

The contingency of uniformed officers dragged the Chevelle driver out of his seat, slapped the cuffs on him after the obligatory pat down and shoved him into the back seat of the nearest cruiser. Sheriff's deputy, 9-1-2, notified dispatch of the Code 4.

Bennett, last to arrive and not part of the physical arrest, asked the driver why he didn't stop. Without hesitation, the driver, a clean-cut young man of about 20, said, "I have a condition that causes blackout spells and I felt one coming on. I was trying to get to the hospital before I passed out."

All the officers looked at each other in utter amazement wishing there was something in addition to misdemeanor traffic charges they could arrest the young man with to keep him off the roads.

*****

Not all police traffic stops involve violations. Sometimes, when conditions are safe, officers will "red light" a civilian friend just for fun. Wearing sun glasses and a hat pulled down over the eyes, it can be very intimidating and frightening to hear a uniformed cop say words to the effect, "You're under arrest, dirtbag. Keep your hands where I can see them or I'll blow you away." This command, of course, must instantly be followed by laughter and some friendly language to make sure the "friend" knows who you are.

******

As a rookie officer my FTO wanted me to gain experience observing traffic violations and writing tickets. Early one evening, we parked in an advantageous location in order to monitor a stop sign. The sign was more of a traffic control device than a safety measure and many driver just slowed down rather than coming to a full stop. We were in plain view of the sign and I was instructed to pull over the first vehicle that failed to come to a complete stop. About the third car lit my red lights. It was a cold day and the driver, an older lady, rolled her window down part way. I told her why I was stopping her and asked her for her operator's license and registration. She tried to convince me she really was in a hurry and was very sorry for not stopping at the sign. I told her my sergeant told me I had to write the ticket, but I would do so as quickly as possible. She then told me she had just taken a laxative and was trying to get home as fast as she could. I reiterated my orders and, documents in hand, re-entered the squad car and began to write the ticket.

After completing the Uniform Traffic Code Citation form, the sergeant told me to run her name, social security number and license plate through the dispatcher for any wants or warrants – just for practice. The systems were slow and it took another twenty minutes or so.

Finished with the computer check and the ticket, I approached the stopped car. As the elderly lady rolled her window down to receive the citation, there was a most distinct and familiar odor permeating the interior of the vehicle. I really felt bad, but the sergeant and I both had a short guilty laugh.

****

April first might not be the first day of summer, but it always seems like it should be. The month of showers that bring May flowers is also the start of the baseball season, Easter, Passover and the anticipation of fair weather. For Detectives Mell Prince and Carl Reicher, it was a day to finally close a series of burglaries that had plagued the small city of Norwood, Ohio.

Acting on a tip, the plain clothes officers hid in the back of a closed for the night jewelry store. Sometime in the early hours of that unofficial first day of summer, two men forced the rear door of this mom and pop business. Both cops commenced firing killing one and seriously wounding the other.

The survivor, one Homer T. Zucker, MW 43, upon recovering from his wounds, was locked up to face burglary charges. At trial and though the Judge was sympathetic to the defense's outrage, Mr. Zucker got the maximum sentence.

Defense lawyer: "Before the officers opened fire did they identify themselves as police officers?"

Homer T. Zucker: "No sir."

Lawyer: "Did they say you were under arrest or tell you not to move?"

Homer T.: "No sir. "

Lawyer: "Did they say anything?"

Homer T.: "Yes sir."

Lawyer: "Well, what did they say?"

Homer T.: "April Fool, dirtbags."

****

Sometime well after midnight, I noticed a late model car parked deep in the shadows of the Terrace Park Swim club. The club closes at dark and this vehicle wasn't there last time I drove by and thus got my attention. Turning my headlights out, I rolled up to the car. While making a visual inspection of the vehicle, I could hear splashing and laughing in the club's pool. Advising dispatch I was two-seven, I used the key on the cruiser's key chain to open the gate into the club's pool area. Though it was very dark, I crept around the building, 4-cell KelLite in hand.

Almost tripping over a pile of clothes at the pool's edge, I spotlighted two teen-agers, sans swim suits, frolicking in the water. Upon identifying myself as a police officer, the guy had no problem complying with my command to get out of the pool. The girl, submerged to her neck, said she wasn't going to get out in front of me. I told her I had all night and it might be less embarrassing if she came out now before other officers arrived. I was working alone, but if the dispatcher didn't hear from me in about five minutes and was then unable to raise me on the radio, he'd begin sending units from adjacent communities to investigate.

She thought it over for a few seconds and then climbed out in the full beam of my flashlight. After they dressed, I made them show me how they got into the fenced pool area so I could make a report to the club. Though they were trespassing, they were local kids and, I sent them on their way with a stern warning.

****

It's easy to keep your cool when you carry a badge and gun. Sometimes being cool is being able to keep things from escalating without having to resort to making an arrest or using force. On an off night, fellow officer Robbie Rezor and I stopped for a drink at one of the area hot spots. This is a bar whose clientele, barkeeps and waitresses are white – as I am. Robbie's black face and short afro stood out like a crow on a snow drift. Not wrong or out-of-place, just stark.

We had no trouble being served, and most patrons didn't register any notice of us. The exception was the adjacent all-male table who almost immediately began making crude, racist comments. Not enough to cause a disturbance, but pointedly directed to us. We had intended to talk shop and our mutually favorite sports teams while enjoying a drink. Being armed meant a one drink limit. However, the guys next to us didn't seem to be nursing their drinks, thus we decided to find a friendlier place to continue our conversations.

As we passed the table of loud mouths, one made a particularly vulgar comment. Robbie stopped next to this punk, and never taking his eyes from the jerk, pulled his off-duty gun from a pocket with his right hand, transferred it to his left hand and placed the pistol in a pocket on his left side. Bravado and insults at this table suddenly vaporized.

Robbie then said in a soft voice, "We'll be waiting outside . . . sonny."

By the time we got to the door, the table of punks hadn't moved, but we didn't wait. Sometimes flashing the blue steel rather than the chrome tin can make a strong point. Robbie, always cool, finished out his LE career with the FBI.

Chapter 17
THEY'RE OUT THERE

Billy Charles just had to kill something. On the way back to his single-wide with carport, depression from the morning's rejection had swelled up in him and was now overwhelming. The only game in season were groundhog, but that required too much patience. He didn't have the nerves today to sit at the edge of an open field and hope to spot a rodent. He wanted to kill now, and it didn't make any difference what.

The Colt AR15, lying under the couch, would be the ticket for release of his anger. Maybe a nice big buck or doe, and if a Game Warden happened to stumble upon the kill, he just might bag him, too. Nobody was going to mess with Billy Charles Conner today.

He grabbed the rifle, extra ammo, his Gerber hunting knife and the forty-five pistol – just in case – and slunk into the woods. Though he believed the Jew bastard Silverstein had chiseled and Jewed his grandfather out of the 210 acre farm in southwestern Indiana, leaving just a half acre and the mobile home, he still considered it his family's farm. To Billy Charles these were "his" woods, and if they ever tried to stop him from hunting here, he'd blow 'em away. He had to take time to think. And walking with a rifle in one hand and a pistol and knife on his side always allowed him to think best, especially if he was on the prowl.

Game, much less legal game, is seldom plentiful at midday, and all he could flush was a robin and a cardinal. Chirping their sing-song warnings to the other animals of the woods, they flew ahead of him, mocking his slow progress. Maybe he should have brought a shotgun instead. The robin landed on the upper most branch of a tall cedar, still singing. He stopped, listening and watching to see if any other creatures were stirring. The robin sang and Billy brought the assault rifle to his shoulder.

The thought occurred to him that maybe the robins were the Jews of the forest. They seemed to always be flitting about, making a lot of noise, stealing this and that to build nests and eating worms – worms he needed as fish bait.

The first shot echoed through the stands of cedar and second growth hardwoods. The robin casually moved on. Though his nearest neighbor was over a quarter mile away, rifle shots carried a long distance. Gunshots, however, were a common sound in the sparsely populated reaches of Southern Indiana, and he had no fear of anyone reporting his. The sound and recoil of the high power long-gun invoked a feeling of mental calmness while at the same time stimulating his heartbeat. The missed shot only made the need to dominate, to show who's boss – to kill – more acute. He changed direction, and now more at ease, stalked deeper into the underbrush.

Within a few hundred yards, and near the northern property line, he settled under the shade of a large ash tree. Billy was aware of his limited formal education, but he also knew he was a lot smarter than others thought he was. He knew that men, country or city people alike, sometimes didn't steal, rob or murder to put food on the table. They stole, robbed and killed because they wanted to. He might not know all the fancy words and psychological reasons, but he believed there was a tremendous and deep rage smoldering in a great portion of the population, himself included. He knew that men who could get food handouts and free rent, committed crimes because they couldn't earn more than the worth of the government gratuities. He had gotten his fill of being just a number, of standing in line, of not being his own person in control and in charge of his fate. Every time he had to collect his allotment of food stamps he had the almost uncontrollable need to prove his worth – to earn respect. Important rich people could surely snuff out a loser like him. Well, he wasn't a loser.

Even with the power of life and death in his hand, Billy Charles felt very small and insignificant. The sadness of losing the chance to reach his future because of bad luck and uncaring employers had crushed his spirit. He had set out to kill something. Maybe he was that something. He lay the rifle at his side and pulled out the government surplus forty-five. It would be easy. There would be no pain. He might be superior to Blacks and Jews, but he was no match for the important and rich men that controlled the world. The humiliation of his family losing this land and having to live out of a used trailer was almost too much to bear.

He examined the weapon from the front end as his thumb coiled around the trigger. Better to die now by his own doing than at the cruel and torturous hand of the government.

Craaack. The second shot of the day reverberated across the hills and valleys, and a starling dropped to the forest floor. Billy Charles felt better. If the robins, reasoned Billy Charles, were the Jews of the woods, the starlings were the niggers. They were the ungrateful and dirty birds that hogged the feed he put out for the other birds, and then messed all over his truck. Well, there was one less today, and if he was going to kill anything it wasn't going to be Billy Charles Conner, not unless he took a few 'robins' and 'starlings' with him.

The forty-three year old bulky animal of a man walked out of the forest and into the sunshine full of self confidence. An hour in the woods and killing something – anything – can do wonders for the soul of a person with a sick mind. The euphoria lasted until he entered his hovel. Killing harmless birds was not akin to spilling the blood of a human. Nobody took notice of dead game.

He spent the rest of the afternoon cleaning guns and putting his survival pack of food and water in order – just in case. For dinner he heated some left over groundhog stew and washed it down with the last of the beer. That night he again read *The Turner Diaries*.

Sunday, around four, he strapped his Gerber to his belt and tucked the semi-auto into his only clean pair of jeans before slipping on a canvas long-rider coat. Into the well used, but clean, F-150 pick-up, he stowed the AR15 and all the ammo he had behind the seat. He loaded the five-gallon jerri-can he kept for emergencies in the truck bed, took a deep breath, and hit the road.

Billy Charles's plan was to drive to the city and commit as much mayhem, death and destruction as he could before having to kill himself. Only problem was, he didn't consciously know this was his plan.

Charlie Rinehart was lucky to be working the day-watch even though his beat was in the less affluent part of the city. Monitoring TOOPs is what he called it – keeping tabs on those who were Temporarily Out Of Prison. Since the bleeding hearts and certain minority cry babies had been down on cops' use of other graphic terms of endearment such as 'dirtbag', 'scumball', 'sleezebag', the police fraternity came up with more descriptive nomenclature to identify those who are, shall we say, recidivistic. Not all TOOPs return to prison, but a significant portion, perhaps the majority, want to be in a place where they get three squares, bed and a roof. Therefore, once their sentence is served, and knowing (hoping?) they will be caught, plan their capers that uncaringly ruin other people's lives. The exception to this common criminal element is the super-predator – a psycho who would rather die than go to jail. Reasoning, threats of arrest or even death mean nothing to this animal-minded man. Persons whose paths they cross seldom remain alive.

Super-predators – losers with nothing to lose – can't be bluffed, intimidated or controlled.

Charlie was the type of cop who tended to search for the good in people. With a noble excuse or sob story, it was usually easy for one to talk him out of a ticket. Over 50 and over 50 pounds overweight, his perennial smile made his presence friendly and reassuring at any gathering . . . or donut shop. Today, he hoped to see his friend the Rabbi, another person who always searched for the good in mankind. Hitching his belt containing the issued .357 Magnum which he had never fired in the line of his 23 years of duty, he ambled toward 7th Street.

Rabbi Stuart Weisenthal, whose parents had been victims of the Nazi Holocaust, considered himself fortunate to have been smuggled to America at age five. Once here he was raised by an uncle and upon graduating from public high school was accepted into the Hebrew Union College.

Seeking solace in his vast collection of books, he scanned the shelves for something to lift the weight of the day's demands. The writings, some new and some very old, told of trials and plights of the Jews from the earliest of times. When it comes to fighting and wars the Jews, a peace loving breed, have little history, save the last fifty years of Israeli warfare. Of all the Jewish holidays, holy days and festivals, the only one that celebrates a battle is Chanukah. How much different was Judas Maccabee's ordeal in the year 165 B.C.E.? Here, after years of slaughter and persecution, he stood to fight the Syrian Greeks – the battle where the eternal light miraculously burned for eight days on one-day's fuel.

Were the victims of the Warsaw Ghetto any less brave? Or the courage of the first Israeli soldiers in combat for the future of Israel of a reduced bravado? These warriors, in the end, as with all Jews, be it in battle or in old age, had one common wish: to die with the holy words of The Shema on their lips.

Late in the afternoon, he realized he must hurry if he was to catch his counterpart and good friend, Father Hogan for their usual Sunday theological discussions. A long time practice both gleaned material for their respective weekly sermons. This week it was the Rabbi's turn to cross the street to the St. Peter in Chains Cathedral. His favorite hand-knitted Yakima atop his head, he locked the door on the 7th street side of the 120 plus year old temple and turned toward the sidewalk.

The first things he saw were six persons. Closest to him and facing toward him was Billy Charles. A few parking spaces west the Jonathan C. Bonhan family had just parked their late model sedan. J.C., as he was known, had exited to the sidewalk and was holding the door for his two, tow-headed pre-teen children. Terri, his wife, was stepping out from the passenger side onto the street. About a half a block or so further west his friend, Patrolman Rinehart, was approaching.

The Bonham family was headed to Music Hall, a few streets to the north, to attend the Cincinnati Symphony Orchestra's Sunday performance. J.C., a physically fit forty something, managed a very profitable upscale restaurant in one of the suburban locations close to his brand new apple-pie, two-story home.

From across the street, as if on cue, the bells of St. Peter in Chains Cathedral chimed the hour.

If you're ever in a situation where another person is about to murder you, at that moment, you'd trade all your worldly possessions for a firearm. And, if that threat was to kill your child or your grandchild, you'd sell your soul for a gun.

The man with a skullcap who almost barged into him had to be a Jew. Billy Charles, an evil hatred glinting in his eyes, couldn't believe his luck. His right hand, the one with the eagle tattooed on it, clasped the Gerber, he moved that half step forward thrusting the knife up an into the chest cavity, splintering bones and savagely ripping the left lung. Bright red blood spurted out from the released diaphragm pressure covering Conner's hand and shirt front. With a savage twist just like the twist of his mouth he yanked it out. Bewilderment, surprise and terror shown on the Rabbi's face as he clutched his upper body. Sinking to his knees, Rabbi Stuart Weisenthal began the chant, "Shema Yisraeil, Adonai . . . ."

Billy Charles, wiping the blade on the shoulder of the mumbling Rabbi, felt power and confidence – he was somebody! Well-practiced at handling weapons, he had the knife sheathed and the rifle unslung as he focused on the movements in front of him.

The struggle just to his east caught J.C.'s eye, and though he always prided himself on being in condition yellow, the threat didn't register. Mr. and Mrs. Boham, both members of the Second Amendment Foundation, not only owned firearms, but each always carried a concealed handgun when working the restaurant or anytime in public.

There's lots worse things than being killed by some thug – one is: watching a family member die at the hands of this thug because you were to much of a fool – or coward – to carry a gun.

Officer Rinehart hadn't survived all these years protecting himself and others not to have noticed a violent act when within his view. Even on such a peaceful Sunday street, he was reaching for his service revolver. It was akin to an old west shoot-out inasmuch as from 100 feet or so two armed men blazed away at each other. One hundred feet or so is a long way for accurate shooting with a four-inch barreled handgun, while almost being point blank range for an AR15. Charlie, facing his death threat only got off two shots, both into the sidewalk, as he fell face forward.

J.C., shoving his children back into the car while pulling his 9mm pistol, was much closer and would be a greater threat than LEO Rinehart except for the expertise of the crazed cop-killer. Billy Charles picked up his new threat and was swinging the assault rifle toward J.C. even before the father of two's Browning Hi-power reached battery.

Terri, on the street side of the car and protected by the vehicle, instinctively retrieved her Charter Arms .38 Special. Thoroughly horrified by the screams of her children and her husband dropping from sight as continuous gunfire continued, she threw her arms over the rooftop and, as trained to do, lined up her sights on Billy Charles.

Simultaneous to identifying the new threat on the far side of the car, Billy Charles's last observation was the sensation of bullets slamming into his chest as Terri emptied the two-inch revolver into him.

They're out there and all the rules, statutes, restraining orders, 911 calls, hand to hand combat techniques, aerosol spray Mace or other pseudo protective measures will never equal the effectiveness of a firearm when faced with an unwarranted and deadly criminal attack.

140

Chapter 18
SOME EASY, SOME NOT SO EASY

Domestic violence calls are the most feared, not so much from possible assaults on the investigating officers by the perp, but also by the complainant. When a man and woman, usually one or both drunk, get into a tussle that turns ugly enough that the law is called, it can be most volatile. Responding officers – plural as a lone cop is at a disadvantage – can be at great peril while trying to sort out the trouble. Oft times the person who made the call will turn on the police if they think their spouse is not being treated nicely. Now it's both belligerents against the LEOs.

Such was the case when John and I found ourselves in the kitchen of an old and trashed two-story on Marion Road. Also crowded in this small room was a very drunk and abusive couple. The woman had called to say her husband, Benny, had been beating her. Making an arrest was always a last resort as usually it would just be a he said/she said confrontation in Mayor's court – which the Mayor would most often dismiss. The first order of business was to separate the combatants and then try to establish some sort of peace. If we were successful, we would end the detail with the threat that if we were called to the house again, somebody was going to jail.

In the Marion Road house the woman kept telling John to keep his hands off of her as he ushered her into the living room. My task was to calm the man down and get his side of the story. Without warning, Benny picked up a carving knife from under a newspaper that was lying on the table, saying, "He better not be hurting' my wife." Benny advanced toward John, whose back was to us. John didn't hear the threat due to the wife's shouting and a TV blaring in the living room.

Use of force is a subjective, you-had-be-there circumstance. Surely a police officer's life was in imminent danger and would justify the use of deadly force against this threat. However, a police officer is fully and solely responsible for each bullet that leaves his gun barrel. If I elected to shoot this possible cop killer and the bullet missed and hit his wife or another person, or the bullet went through the target with the same end results, I could be held criminally liable. This decision of life and death, based on 6th and 7th senses, must be made instinctively and instantaneously – unlike after-the-fact court room scrutiny.

My reaction, in addition to shouting, "HE'S GOT A KNIFE," was to take a two-hand hold of my 4-cell aluminum flashlight and reach over the perp's head and pull back against his throat. Too hard and I could crush his larynx, too easy and he could stab me. I managed to knock him to the floor where both John and I jumped on him and seized the knife. Benny's wife, the alleged victim, now leaped on top of all of us.

When things calmed down and Benny and his wife had sobered up a little, they apologized to us. Though we had a case of assault on a police officer, it was near end of shift and both John and I could not see any sense in arresting either one only to have them released with a wrist slap. Neither of them had any felony convictions and had always been easy to get along with – when sober.

******

John and I had another physical confrontation with a man selling rugs by the side of the road. He had been warned and cited previously. This time, however, the Mayor saw him, and taking it as a personal affront, ordered his arrest. The seller, a physically fit 6'1", 190 pound, 20-something man, didn't want to go peacefully. The guy didn't strike at either of us, just resisted. When he refused to place his hands behind his back to be cuffed, we first tried to twist his arms. As he sprung free, John grabbed him in a bear hug as I took hold of his pony tail and yanked as hard as I could. His legs gave out or he just collapsed and the three of us fell to the gravel drive. Not knowing if he was armed, our first concern was his hands. Scrambling around, John and I ended up sitting on him with his arms spread eagled. I put a knee on his head shoving his face into the gravel while holding one arm enabling John to wrench his other arm behind his back. All of us were breathing hard. First one cuff then the other and finally a pat down to check for weapons. Picking someone up by the cuffed hands is most painful, but maybe our prisoner's discomfort was lessened because I used his pony tail to help with the lift. Eventually he accepted the situation and walked to the cruiser. John and I were dirty, bruised and scratched, but he was hurtin' too.

*****

Assaults are part of the risk of any confrontation with persons who resent being caught or told what to do. Even what appears to be simple traffic stops can turn violent such as the time I observed a vehicle weaving down Springfield Pike. At my first opportunity I snapped on the roof lights. The guy, unlike most drivers, ignored me. I blipped the siren a few times. Still no reaction. Now, I advised the dispatcher of the situation as I looked for an opportunity to pull alongside and force him off the road before someone got hurt. Though our vehicles never touched, he finally came to a stop over the curb and on the sidewalk. By this time other officers were arriving and we got the driver out. He seemed to be intoxicated, but I couldn't smell the odor of alcoholic beverage on his breath so I was going to let him go with a ticket. The other officers were all standing around when I presented the citation to the dude. Without any warning, he took a big roundhouse swing at me knocking

143

my hat off and me into the cruiser. Before I could recover the other cops had him against the fender and in cuffs.

At the station, while trying to fingerprint him, he again took another swing at me. This time, while he was held to the floor, one of my fellow officers sprayed the perp's face with Mace. It didn't faze him, but we all had teary eyes. Because he was physically arrested and his car was on the public roadway, we towed it to our impound lot and during an inventory search discovered a few bags of Mary Jane. He might not have been DUI on alcohol, but he sure was under the influence of the marijuana.

The court, finding him guilty of two counts of assault on a police officer and possession of an illegal substance, gave him 180 days.

About seven months later, while on patrol, I noticed a vehicle behind me flashing his headlights. Thinking some citizen needed help, I pulled over and got out of my scout car. The driver got out of his car and I immediately recognized him as the man who had assaulted me. As he started toward me, I put my hand on my gun and told him to stop. This time he froze while saying he only wanted to apologize. Police officers, on duty and in uniform can't afford, prima facie, to put their trust in anyone. I made him return to his vehicle while I radioed for backup, code 2. With another officer present, we questioned him. He reiterated his want to say how sorry he was for his behavior earlier that year. I didn't know nor will ever know of his sincerity – or care.

*****

Coming over the radio, as I walked into the squad room at the start of my second shift, was an all-county broadcast:

"Wanted by the Hamilton County Sheriff's Office for rape of a minor is one male black, 20 to 25 years of age, approximately six feet tall, 160 pounds and driving an older model convertible, blue in color. Subject is believed to go by the name of Curly. Offense occurred 1300 hours this date. Authority Hamilton County SO."

It was like the muzzle flash of a handgun during night training. I had had contact with such a suspect just days ago and I knew where he lived. I told my shift officer of my suspicions and he authorized over-time for the day officer to accompany me to check Curly's home. Within minutes, we found the address – with a blue convertible parked in front. It was a warm and sunny afternoon and there were four guys leaning on or around this car. I recognized the subject and, after parking the scout car, approached the guys. To Curly, I said, "How ya doin' Curly. You have a date with a pretty young girl a little while ago?"

He grinned and nudged one of his buddies, "Yeah. How you know about it?"

"It seems she told a Sheriff's Deputy that you forced your intentions on her. She was also under age."

"Ah man, how was I to know how old she was. Besides, she was asking for it," Curly whined.

I had met Curly a few days previous when he reported the theft of a stereo from his blue convertible. Though the name on his driver's license was Charlton, he mentioned that he went by the name of Curly.

"Perhaps you can straighten this out, and I'm sorry we have to do this in front of your buddies, but we have to take you in because there's a warrant out for you," I said, pulling out my handcuffs. He knew the routine, placing his hands on the hood of the car and spreading his legs for the obligatory pat down.

We took mug shots and prints while waiting for a deputy to claim him. By 1800 hours the dispatcher had put out a cancel on the earlier broadcast ending with the comment that Woodlawn had picked up the suspect and turned him over to the Sheriff's Department. This had to be the easiest felony collar I ever made.

****

Driving While Intoxicated, like felony arrests, always demand backup. Some inebriants become friendly, some mean and violent and some just pass out. Drunks with priors and without money, insurance or a license tend to resort to violence – they know what's in store for them. Once restrained, they usually cop a plea and do a month or so in the slammer and then start all over again. The first timer, especially a prominent citizen, is compliant, secure in the knowledge their lawyer will get them off.

To the arresting officer, it's always a perfect case – see erratic driving, smell the odor of alcoholic beverage on the offender's breath and watch as this drunk fails the field sobriety tests. Blood tests (and now breathalyzers) are just extra proof.

I watched a newer model Chevrolet pull out of Novner Drive onto Springfield Pike forcing another car to swerve to avoid an accident. I pulled in behind the Chevy and immediately tripped the roof lights. The guy wove back and forth between the lanes before finally pulling into the parking lot of the Mill Creek Saloon. He got about half way into a parking spot right in front before stopping. Backup had already arrived and we had no trouble getting this very inebriated man out of his car. He was so drunk he had trouble understanding the commands to touch his nose with his finger and walk a straight line. This well dressed middle-aged guy put up no resistance as we took him to the station and booked him. Turns out he was a well-known doctor in another part of the county and we released him on an OR bond to his wife.

Chalk up another good bust. It was, until we got to court. Here, the doctor's lawyer produced the waitress of the Mill Creek Saloon who stated, under oath, she had refused to continue to serve the doctor because she believed he was drunk. She then stated that in a short period of time after that, she was attracted to the flashing red lights in the parking lot and saw the doctor, whose car was half out of a parking place, being arrested.

The doctor, testified that he never left the parking lot. He said I turned on my red lights as he was backing out of the parking space and never drove on the street. The judge, the prosecutor and the lawyer conferred agreeing that if the doctor would sign a release not to sue me or the agency, he would be found not guilty.

The next night, on a hunch, I stopped in to Cupid's Bar and Grill on Novner Drive and asked the bartender if he knew the doctor, and had he seen him on the night of the arrest. Yes, the doctor was a regular and he remembered the night because not only had he had refused to serve the doctor believing him to be well past the limit, but he saw me red light him.

What had happened was; the doctor, being refused further service at the Mill Creek bar, got in his car, drove the two blocks to Cupid's, was refused service and when red-lighted, pulled back into the same parking spot he had left only a few minutes previous. The waitress was telling the truth – that she refused him additional drinks and within a few minutes looked out to see the doctor being placed under arrest. Being busy, she wasn't aware of the exact time span of when he left his table or when she noticed him being arrested. Therefore, it was possible the doctor had been the victim of an over-zealous police officer who was just trying to keep a obviously drunk driver off the highway.

Of course, had we known his defense, we would have subpoenaed the barkeep from Cupid's to support the fact that the MD had driven on the public road. There is also the possibility the doctor might, also, have been telling the truth inasmuch as he was so drunk he didn't remember his little trip to Cupid's.

****

"Can you develop and print photos?" the Chief asked as I walked into the station to begin my second shift.

"Yeah, sure. What do you need, Chief?" Well, I really hadn't developed and printed photos, personally. However, I had watched Amberley Patrolman and photo officer, Robbins, and he had promised to teach me in their dark room. The Chief knew I carried a Minox camera on my duty belt and had used it to take pics of auto accidents and thus might have assumed I had my own dark room. Who was I, a lowly patrolman, to challenge the thoughts of our head LEO.

It seems there had been a burglary on third shift and the prosecutor's office needed prints of the crime scene before the preliminary hearing the next day. I told the Chief I didn't have my own darkroom, but I was sure I could use the facilities at Amberley Village. A phone call to APD confirmed that Robby was working and would show me the ropes. I took a marked patrol car and told the dispatcher, "4-6-8-B, 2-7 out of territory."

Three hours later I turned in a stack of prints and, with the admiration of the Chief, became the de facto department photographer. Prior to inheriting the responsibility for the agency's photos, the dark room work had been done by a neighboring police department. In order to use photographs in court proceedings there must be a chain of evidence. In other words, the photographer and the person who develops and prints the images must be available to testify that they did not alter or tamper with the photos and that the property was never out of their possession. Also, because black & white film was used almost exclusively, the photographer might be called upon to explain how photographs of, for example, a red substance such as blood, could be conclusively shown in a B&W photo.

Within a few months, Woodlawn sent me to a Kodak police photography class in Hocking Hills, Ohio. From this and my experiences with the Minox camera, I wrote an article for one of the police magazines. This led to my appointment as the Police Photography Instructor for the Norwood, Ohio Police Academy.

As officers retire or move on, sometimes departments are left without a camera much less an officer that knows how to take proper evidence photos. A situation such as this occurred in neighboring Lincoln Heights during a murder investigation. I responded to their call for a crime scene photographer and took shots of a very dead dude lying face down in the middle of a street. The OIC believed the killing had taken place elsewhere and the body dumped from a car. He based his observations on the fact that there was almost no blood on the street under the victim's body. The dude had a significant wound to the chest and his ear had been sliced in half – also with no blood on that side of his head or ear. I pointed out the possibility that he had been stabbed in the chest – right through the heart - and was dead before the slash to his ear. Thus, his heart had stopped pumping at the instant of being pierced and therefore all blood flow ceased. The coroner confirmed my analogy and Lincoln Heights focused on the street as the only crime scene. Through excellent investigative work they caught the killer.

Chapter 19
OFFICER NEEDS ASSISTANCE

Alarm drops, especially on a Sunday, are almost always false alarms or the result of a power failure. An exception to the "almost always" rule happened in the Village of Woodlawn, Ohio at the Metal Fabricating Company one sunny, calm spring morning.

There're called drops because a sudden drop in electric power triggers them – such as when the circuit is broken by a severed wire, opened door or window. Most system's alarm activations are sent to the alarm company by phone wire. The alarm company then forwards the location to the appropriate police agency who then radios the beat officer for that jurisdiction. Some alarm systems distinguish between intrusion (burglary), robbery or panic. The latter two usually require intentional activation such requiring a person to deliberately push a button.

"Four-six eight, car 4-6-8, alarm drop the Metal Fabrication Company, 423 Novner Drive, Car 4-6-8."

Since false alarms are common, there was no urgency in the dispatcher's voice – just routine. Patrolman Tom McDaniel, running the primary beat car 4-6-8, acknowledged the call and turned his squad car toward the industrial park of this small suburban town. His backup, Lt. Webster, 4-7-0, was just finishing a coffee break and would also respond, just in case.

Arriving at MFC, Tom immediately sensed something wrong. There was a tan over puke green losermobile backed up to the loading dock with the trunk lid and driver's door standing open. Stopping at the head of the drive entrance, and before he could key the mic to request backup, a man climbed out of what appeared to be a hole in the closed garage door. Tom sprang out of the cruiser and reached for his sidearm. The guy, wearing work clothes, held up his hands as he walked around his car.

Perhaps this was just a maintenance employee who had accidently set off the alarm. The middle aged man, still with his hands in the air, was now next to the open driver's door. McDaniel drew his Smith and Wesson revolver and ordered the man to stop. He didn't. Instead he reached under the front seat, pulled a semi-auto pistol, spun around and opened fire.

Tom reacted as he had been trained. Using the cover of the cruiser door he returned fire. Bullets thudded against the cruiser's fenders and doors, glass sprayed him and he realized he'd been hit. Ignoring the pain in his arm, his three-fifty-seven magnum now empty, he ejected the spent shells and in a continuing motion dumped the contents of his spare cartridge pouch into his hand. The pouch contained ammo, but also coins and a stick of chewing gum. Cursing under his breath for using this pouch for non-ammunition items, he picked the cartridges from among the other debris while continuing to glance from behind the door to check on his assailant. The man in working clothes was in a sort of sitting, lounging position, his back against the door sill. The shooting had stopped – at least for the moment. Not knowing if his assailant was two-seven or if there were accomplices waiting to open fire, patrolman McDaniel took advantage of the lull. The hair on the nape of his neck fully raised, he turned his back to grab the mic.

Training is paramount to handling firearms. Being brave and calm enough to put that training to use when facing a lethal attack is what makes heroes.

"FOUR-SIX-EIGHT SHOTS FIRED, MFC CORP-ORATION, NOVNER DRIVE, I'M HIT." He dropped the mic and put his full concentration on the car, the shooter who tried to kill him and the search for others who might also be a danger. He didn't know if his radio transmission had gotten out. He had six shots in his Model 19 and six more – plus change – in the second pouch. Retreating was not an option.

"All cars stand-by. 4-6-8 requesting assistance, shots fired, MFC Corporation, 423 Novner Drive, Woodlawn, Ohio. All cars in the vicinity respond code three. Car 4-7-0. . . ."

The most dreaded calls a cop can hear is officer needs assistance and I'm hit or officer down. All LEOs within a few minutes of the location, regardless of the jurisdiction they represent or what they are doing, instinctively switch on red lights and sirens and speed as fast as they dare to help a brother officer.

Tom, bleeding from a wound on his arm and not taking his eyes from the now motionless form twenty or so yards to his front, crouched behind his door and wisely waited for the backup.

The Lieutenant, the first to arrive, and sensing the situation, pulled his vehicle across the lawn and between McDaniel's car and the beater. He secured a shotgun from the trunk, racked a round of double-ought buck into the chamber and took cover next to Tom. Seeing blood on the patrolman's arm, the Lt. radioed for the life squad. He did not put out a code four as the area was not secure and it was unknown if the perp, who had not moved, was out of commission or if there were others that posed a threat. Additional patrol cars, sirens shrieking, soon began arriving.

Within minutes the front, back and sides of the factory were surrounded by uniformed, riot gun toting officers. Approaching the downed shooter, who was slacked-jawed, eyes vacant and with an obviously significant head wound, Lt. Webster bent to hear what sounds were coming from the perp's mouth. Hearing only guttural death throes, The Lt.

slammed the butt of his shotgun into the cop-killer wannabe screaming, "SHUT UP SCUM!"

Because this was before SWAT or tactical teams had been organized, the Lt. implemented a full search of the building with officers from four different agencies. If there had been accomplices, they were not to be found. Woodlawn officer Tom McDaniel, luckily, was not seriously injured, but one of his shots had struck the perp in the head. He was DOA.

The burglar, with a long criminal history, had cut a man sized hole in the company's loading dock door Then from the trunk of his car, pulled an acetylene torch hose into the building where he was cutting the company safe open when he inadvertently tripped the alarm. Knowing he was facing a long stretch in the pen, he obviously thought he could shoot his way out against a lone cop – especially from a distance of at least twenty yards. Up against a police officer who was not afraid to engage in a firefight and who remained calm enough to put his training into practice – the perp figured wrong, dead wrong.

The coroner's office located the dirtbag's wife in West Virginia. She refused to claim the body.

> *"Woodlawn PD had high firearms training standards for the time. When I joined the Department I struggled to meet those standards, but Lt. Webster never let up on me and I finally met those standards after about 2 months of relentless training. Needless to say, I'm here because of the Lt's dedication." T.R. McDaniel 28 Dec 10*

Tom McDaniel worked a few more years for Woodlawn before hiring on with the City of Blue Ash, Ohio. Here he became one of the most respected detectives in Hamilton County. Tom finished out his police career as Chief of Police for Harrison, Ohio.

Chapter 20
THE SPIRIT OF THANKSGIVING

"Omar? Now listen to me and be sure you get a nice big fat one. Do you hear me?" The shrill woman's voice chased him all the way to the truck.

He didn't need to answer. After 17 years he could tell the rhetorical advice and questions from the important ones. He just hoped the little pick-up would make it out back of Mason City to the turkey farm. Ever since his son had become interested in hot rodding the old truck had not been the same. Of all things, the V8 now had two carburetors on it! The gas consumption had to be twice as high and it didn't seem to start as easily as it used to. He wished Jeff had spent his money and time fixing things that really needed fixing - like the radiator. It had leaked for at least a year and necessitated the carrying of a can of water at all times.

Remembering that Jeff had been the last to drive the six-year-old '49 Ford he climbed back out of the cab to check the jerri-can which was always kept in the bed. It aggravated him that the can, formerly a standard issue gas can that he had "requisitioned" from his jeep at the reserve unit, was near empty. Jeff was very negligent about such things but he had to admire his son's ability to work on cars. Omar filled the container with water adding a generous amount of Radiator Glycerine anti-freeze, in case it turned colder.

It wasn't a pretty morning but promised to turn out fine if the sun could break through the thin high blanket of clouds. For Eastern Kentucky it was a typical Thanksgiving Day and perfect for a drive to the country.

He loafed along the twisty, hilly roads in no particular hurry to get to Cotton's Turkey farm. The trip, two counties north, should take about an hour or so each way plus a half hour to select and have slaughtered the evening meal. Along about midway, on a stretch of two lane road that the county had failed to blacktop, the old faithful flathead quit. It sputtered a few times and a jab at the accelerator pedal caused a spurt of power but in a few turns of the tires it stopped, right smack in the middle of nowhere.

A cursory look at the engine showed no obvious signs of problems. He removed one of the small chrome racing style air cleaners and checked for fuel from the accelerator pump while he worked the throttle linkage by hand. Nothing. He was sure the gas tank was not empty as the gauge indicated about three-quarters full. From the side of the road he broke the stalk of a now dried thistle, inserted it into the gas filler pipe and confirmed this. Removing the fuel filter exposed the problem - dirt! Ten minutes and a few bars whistled of "As time goes by" and he was repositioning the cleaned sediment bowl oblivious to the car that had pulled up behind him.

"Having a little trouble, pal?" The pot-bellied Sheriff demanded, adjusting his holster and gun, as he approached Omar.

"I think I've got it fixed now, officer," Omar replied, surprised to see this sloppily uniformed officer.

"You, ain't from around these parts, are you? What are you doin' here anyway? You got a partner off in the woods stealin' from some poor farmer or poachin' game?" The gun toter accused.

"Why no sir. I . . . my truck just developed a dirty fuel filter and I was cleaning . . . ."

"A likely story. We've been bothered by you non-residents coming out here to take what you can. Besides, it's against the law to park on the highway. I ought ta tow that heap of yours away and run you in just to make sure you ain't up to no good. But, seein' that it's Thanksgivin' an all,

I'll just fine ya five dollars and let it go at that," the Sheriff ordered, an insincere, semi-toothless smile breaking out on his pudgy, unshaven face.

Catching the drift of the law officer's intentions, Omar, now out from under the hood but careful not to make eye contact, replied in a humble tone, "Why thank you sir. I'll be out of here, lickety-split."

He handed the man a crumpled fin, closed the hood and slid into the cab. Omar watched the Sheriff watch him, as the roof mounted red light oscillated slowly and ominously on the '55 Ford patrol car.

Drained of gas, the engine had to be cranked over many times in order for the fuel pump to refill the float bowls. It took more cranks than the old six-volt battery had in it. Omar was sure he was going to spend Thanksgiving in jail now.

The Sheriff approached the open truck window, curled his upper lip and through a whiskey tainted, putrid, rotted-tooth half smile, belched, "Need a push, pal?"

Phew, maybe the cop, bad breath and misfeasance intentions aside, wasn't such a jerk after all. "It sure looks like it, sir. Mighty neighborly of ya to offer me your kind help."

"That's why the County put push bars on this here patrol car, so as we can be of service to the public. Course it'll cost ya a fiver," the obese badge carrier said with that same insincere sneer.

Omar produced another five spot leaving him with less than ten dollars which he hoped was enough for the object of this trip - the bird.

With a tap and a push the little pick-up sprang to life. Omar waved a good-bye and gingerly drove away not knowing what the speed limit was and fearful of having to deal with the law again.

The Turkey farm was a pleasant experience if witnessing the slaughter of a live animal can ever be pleasant. The men and women who did the work, however, were nice enough. When he explained his tangle with the Sheriff, careful not to be too critical as any of them could be kin to the law man, they all expressed their understanding. They understood alright. This was their county and outsiders better mind their P's and Q's.

It was turning decidedly colder and giant dark, bulbous clouds now threatened snow. With a full radiator, topped off from his jerri-can and the fresh bird carefully wrapped and on the seat next to him, Omar started for home. Mindful of the fact he had only a few dollars left - not enough for any more "fines" - he nonetheless increased his speed in hopes of beating the snow.

It was going to be a swell dinner. His brother, mom, dad and both of his boys would be there for this annual affair. He and Abigail, his wife, had spent the past weekend cleaning and polishing the little two bedroom frame house. It was their first home, bought, just after the war, with the G.I. loan available for returning soldiers. Though he had expected to move to a bigger place closer to the city, they had grown used to the country life and just stayed.

Uh-oh! Deep between mountainous hills, pulled to the side of the road, hood

up, was the Sheriff's car. Too late to turn back on the narrow tree lined road, Omar hoped he could just slip on by with a wave of the hand. Slowing to a crawl, he double-clutched into first gear and racked his brain for a plausible story as to why he had to hurry on.

Abreast of the two-tone brown sedan, the driver stepped in his path, hand raised - palm forward. Dangit now! "Howdy Sheriff. Hope everything is okay. I'd like to stop and talk, but I'm late for Thanksgiving dinner," Omar pleaded.

The Sheriff, his eyes bulging, scanned the interior of Omar's cab, saying, "Now that's no way to talk to a friend who just gave you a push and kept you out of jail. By the looks of that package on your seat I don't think they'll be startin' the dinner without you, will they?" Without waiting for an answer the man with the power of arrest continued. "It seems, ol' buddy, that my scout car has run out of gas and I just might have to declare an emergency and commandeer your truck so as I can get me some."

"Uh . . . sir. Why don't you radio for someone to bring it to you?" Omar sheepishly tendered trying to be helpful without insulting the man.

"Can't. Radio won't reach from down in this hollar and besides, I'm the only one working in the whole county, this bein' a holly-day and all. So why don't . . . ." The Man paused in his command to seize Omar's truck as he noticed the jerri-can in the bed of the pick-up. "Say, you wouldn't be tryin' ta hold out on me now, would-ja?"

"No, sir. What are you talking about?" Omar asked, weighing his options. He could just race away and the fat cop would never be able to catch him or even radio for help. That idea was suppressed as he noticed the Sheriff casually massaging the big revolver on his hip.

"Is that can full? That one there in the back of this here truck?" The Sheriff asked, raising his voice as he reached over the side and shook the can.

"Almost full, Sheriff. Here let me help you, it's kind of dirty," Omar offered scrambling out of the cab. "I plumb forgot about my spare can. I always carry it with me just in case I get between stations.

"Now that's the right spirit. How much do you want for a few gallons? I don't want it all."

"Oh, I wouldn't charge you, being as you have helped me so much today. Besides, if I sold you the contents of this can that would be illegal since I don't have a vendor's license. So if it's okay with you I'll just pour a few gallons into your tank and be on my way."

"Son, you catch on real quick. And just to show you I'm an alright guy I'm not going to notice that olive-drab colored jerri-can has U.S. Government markings on it. And while I'm in a Thanksgiving spirit I'm gonna return that fiver you paid for the push awhile back. Course I can't return the fine for illegal parking - I'm sure you understand; that's County money."

It was a wonderful Thanksgiving. The turkey and trimmings, especially Abigail's pumpkin pie, were perfect. However, Omar, thankful as he was, felt a twinge of hypocritical guilt during the dinner prayer, but only a small one.

Chapter 21
SHERIFFIN'

With conditions perfect for reading the Sunday paper, no plans, dreary light rain and the need to catch up on some rest, I settled deep into my favorite chair. Before I could finish the funnies, the all-too-familiar ring of a phone jarred me from the complacency of the morning.

"Deputy Klein?" The voice had a sense of urgency to it.

"Yes, this is Special Deputy Klein."

"Sir, this is Howard Kadison with the Delta Queen Steamboat Company in New Orleans. I was given your number by the Sheriff's Department. I'm trying to find the *Mississippi Queen,* which, I believe or hope, is at the boat ramp just up river from Patriot. I've been unable to reach them by radio-phone and I'm hoping you can help me."

"Hold on a second," I said. "And I'll look out my window. I can see the area, which is about a half mile from here." My farm lay along both sides of the Goose Creek which was really, a navigable bay off the Ohio River just upstream from Patriot, Indiana. I looked, but due to rain, fog and full spring foliage, I couldn't see anything resembling a four-story, floating hotel. "No, sir, I can't see the ship. What do you want me to do?"

"Well, aside from finding the boat, I'll need information on how we can get some buses to the location to transport the passengers to the Cincinnati airport. Can this area be reached by large buses? How far away is Cincinnati by road? How much time wise?"

"Wait a minute. One question at a time, please," I interrupted. The caller seemed a little excited, which could be expected of someone who had lost a ship of that caliber. "Now, what's the first priority?"

Mr. Kadison audibly took a deep breath and in a calmer voice asked. "We need to know exactly where the boat is and I must to talk with the Captain."

"Okay. I'll go to the boat ramp and either report back to you myself if the boat's not there, or if it is, I'll bring the Captain back here. Give me your number and half an hour."

Realizing time was critical; I just grabbed my ball cap with Deputy Sheriff emblazoned across the riser. This was the mid-1980s and though I wasn't a full time deputy, I had full police powers. Switzerland County Sheriff J.D. Leap had deputized me so there would be someone in the Patriot area that could certify vehicle titles and be available when needed for other duties and details that arose. The county, about midway between Louisville, Kentucky and Cincinnati, Ohio, was populated by less than 7000 residents. The Sheriff's Office had only eight full time officers which meant that there were times when no one was on duty. The town of Patriot, population about 200, did not employ any LEOs.

Arriving at the ramp, I could now see the magnificent twin stacks of the western style steamboat proudly peeking above a large silver maple. As light rain continued to fall I made my way, slogging through the wet grass and mud, to where the bow was nosed into shore. Within minutes, the crew had lowered a gangway and after identifying myself and requesting to speak with the Captain, I was allowed onboard.

Walking through the galley, there were cheers and light hearted shouts of "we're saved – the Calvary has arrived." Captain Keeton, gold braid and all, was anxious and relieved to learn the company was in touch. On the way back to the house, he told me the ship was taking the passengers, Kentucky Derby fans, from Louisville to Cincinnati where most were to catch a plane. However, because of recent heavy rains the river was running so fast the *Queen* couldn't generate enough speed to reach Cincinnati in time. The Company decided to put ashore at Patriot and bus the passengers the rest of the way. While making the plans marine radio-telephone communication was lost due to the surrounding hills.

Not only would the disembarking passengers have to be bused to their final destination, but all the ship's supplies of food, flowers, produce, clothing and dairy products – and southbound passengers that were waiting in Cincinnati - would have to be transported here. This was a significant logistical mental and physical exercise. While the Captain and Mr. Kadison made plans on my kitchen phone, I used the fire channel on my police portable radio to ask the Patriot Fire Chief, George Miller, to meet me at the ramp. I also took the opportunity to put on my uniform as traffic duties and order-keeping might be needed. Since no one from the Sheriff's office had shown up, I assumed, being a Sunday, no one was on duty, save the jailer/dispatcher.

Upon arriving back at the ramp, I apprised Chief Miller of the situation and he volunteered to set up a tarp to keep the soon to be off-loaded luggage dry. As the Chief put out word of the plight, other volunteer fire department members brought wood pallets to make a walkway over the mud. It took over three hours for all 350 passengers and their luggage to come ashore, some having to walk through intermittent rain.

Once the ship was empty of travelers, the Captain offered the run of the boat to the volunteers including a plea to help eat all the food that would otherwise have to go to waste. Such opulence! This floating four-star hotel has a staff of 150 to care for the every whim of its passengers. While riding the swells, these lucky swells can enjoy a movie, browse the onboard library, or just relax in any of the many finely upholstered leather chairs and sofas. The staterooms ran from the rather spartan inboard cabins, barely larger than a walk-in closet with bunk beds, to the first-class suites on the Promenade Deck. This upper floor (via elevator, no less) contains the crème de la crème of the rooms. Each had a picture window, petite loveseat, two arm chairs and a king-size bed. Above this deck was a small swimming pool and open area for sunbathing. The Observation Deck contained the main salon and dining room with an oblong-shaped crystal chandelier as large as a canoe. Entertainment is made possible by three pianos and two elevated stages, each with complete sound systems. The ship, the largest sternwheeler steamboat in the world, is 382 feet long and 81 feet from the waterline to the top of the telescoping stacks (collapsible to clear low bridges). She draws less than twelve feet of water as that is the minimum depth the U.S. Army Corps of engineers is required to maintain in the Ohio River.

By late afternoon the fun was over with the arrival of the down bound passengers, trucks of supplies and hordes of local sightseers. Sometimes police work is a lot of fun.

****

Because the Sheriff is elected, he and his deputies have the added burden of maintaining a positive public relations image. This is not to say they ignore criminal behavior, just they have to have a soft edge to their hard duties.

One of these catch-more-bees-with-honey/live-and-let-live situations occurred at the farm next to mine. Though a mile away, Sonny was my closest neighbor to the east. He wasn't the owner, only rented the house and two of the 200 acres. I ran into him in the town of Patriot one morning where I mentioned I had heard he was throwing a large "pig" roast that night. He stammered a little and then asked me straight out, as is the custom of country folks, if I was going to cause him any trouble.

This was mid August and I knew Sonny didn't keep any hogs. He worked on the county road crew and like most in this isolated and poor area of Southeastern Indiana was not financially well off. Thus, the "pig" was most likely a deer taken out of season. I played dumb and assured him he could expect no trouble from me – his neighbor. Sonny gave me a big smile and invited me to the roast. Taking game for food was not a serious offense in the eyes of local cops. State police and conservation officers might have had a different view.

Around dusk, my wife and I drove our '41 Jeep that we used as our ATV to Sonny's. The "pig" was just being carved and many of the partiers were drinking beer and maybe other beverages in paper cups. Things quieted down a little when we arrived. Nobody was sure what I was going to do. Sonny came up to me with some "pig" and announced that as his friend and neighbor I wasn't there to cause any trouble. I returned the smile and accepted the tendered, tender roasted meat.

One of the other partiers approached with a cup of a dark liquid on ice and a beer, offering me my choice. I declined the kind offer saying I never drank when I was carrying a gun. We stayed less than an hour, but because I was considered more one of them, than *them,* I received future occasional tips about real crimes.

****

My nearest neighbor to the west, about a half mile, was one of the toughest men I've ever known. Because the property owner lived in Cincinnati, I kept an eye on the farm and farm house by occasionally driving back the quarter mile dirt road to this turn-of-the-century two-story frame former mansion. The stately home was in need of wrecking ball as previous tenants had ripped most of the

164

interior paneling and magnificent curved banister to burn for firewood when their fuel oil ran out.

On one of my inspections, I found a thirtyish beefy man living there with his wife and baby. He told me he was from Iowa and was a Boilermaker who had found work on the new steel plant across the river in Ghent, Kentucky. Parked between the barn and house was his late-model, dual wheel truck outfitted with a generator and welding rig. Behind the truck was a newer Bayliner 22' cabin cruiser on a trailer. Expensive stuff for a guy living in a cheap rental. Of course, seclusion on a dirt road might be of greater value than rent if you're hiding something.

We shook hands and exchanged names – his was Virgil Draper. I told him if there was anything I could do, please let me know as country neighbors always have to look out for each other. I didn't tell him I was a reserve officer with the SO. He, appreciated the gesture and, in turn, offered to do any welding I might need done. He was proud of his equipment and walked me around the vehicles. I made a mental note of the Iowa license plate.

In this sparsely populated county where police, fire and life squads were at least 20 minutes away, neighbors – even if they were feuding – dropped everything and came when help was needed.

Within a few days I ran into Bruce Wilkins, a friend and detective with the Indiana State Police. I passed the information about Mr. Draper along suspecting he might be wanted by someone. Bruce ran the name and plate number through NCIC and we got a hit. Seems an active felony warrant had been issued by authorities in Iowa for a stolen boat and trailer – just like the one I observed hooked to Virgil's truck.

Detective Wilkins asked me if I wanted to be part of the raiding party, but I declined requesting that my name be kept out of the matter. The next day Virgil was busted and the boat impounded. After a week's incarceration in the Rising Sun, Indiana jail, Iowa declined to extradite him and he was freed. Virgil always maintained he had paid for the boat, but the previous owner had not paid the finance company for the lien. Virgil had failed to make the check out to the loan company. This seemed more like a civil matter than a crime and might have been the reason the state refused extradition.

I stopped by the farm house soon after he returned home to find him most distraught. He had been remiss in paying his electric bill and the power company had shut him off. Without electric, his baby's formula was spoiling along with all the other food in the refrigerator. We were standing in the yard next to the electric pole closest to the house and alongside to my '41 farm Jeep. I looked up and seeing the open switch, said, pointing up, "If you could reach the switch, you could turn the power on. All you have to do is figure out how you can get close enough to shut the switch. Do you have a really long ladder?"

Virgil shook his head as he looked in the back of my Jeep and it's collection of wooden handled rakes, shovels, and other implements, and said, "If I climb the pole, will you toss me that iron rake?"

Wood telephone and electric poles that have only been climbed by men with spiked boots, leave a very rough surface. Virgil took a short jump wrapping his arms and legs around the pole. He then shinnied up to within three to four feet of the switch. With one arm around the pole, he called for the rake. I got it to him on the second toss enabling him to close the switch. Sapped of strength from the climb, he slid most of the way down impaling finger sized splinters in his arms, legs and body. Tough guy. He was most grateful and wished he could do something for me. Sure, it was not the most legal action I could have taken, but sometimes the safety and security of a child rules.

While driving through Rising Sun about a month later and very late at night, Virgil was stopped for an alleged minor traffic violation. The officer stopping him was the Chief of Police and was also known as a very tough – and mean – man. This LEO was one of the officers in on the arrest and was not pleased to turn Vigil loose after Iowa refused extradition. The Chief got Virgil out of his truck and then preceded to pistol-whip him. Virgil took a number of deep lacerations before wresting the handgun from the Chief and tossing it away. By this time backup had arrived and my neighbor was arrested again. He was charged with assaulting a police officer and a number of misdemeanor charges. But, tough also means grit when facing the law. He filed charges against the Chief for assault and violation of his civil rights. The FBI conducted an investigation and as a result the fifteen year veteran Chief of Police was forced to resign. Virgil moved on, the former Chief found work as a security officer where, few months later, he committed suicide.

****

There are, of course, some guys who just like to get away with besting LE. I was attending a dance at the fire department with my wife when it was raided by the state liquor agents. Their information was that there would be underage drinking. We were all ushered out while the agents conducted their investigation and search. While standing in the crowd, someone pushed me from behind – hard. I apologized to the couple I was knocked into and then turned around to see who did the pushing. No one owned up.

A month or so later, my neighbor to the east, Sonny, informed me that the pusher was convicted murderer Terry

Bartwell. Ten years prior, Terry had killed his wife with a shotgun blast after learning she was running around on him. He did six years of a 20 year sentence. Knowing my informant would tell others what he had told me, I couldn't let this go or I'd be known as a coward. The opportunity for a confrontation came one afternoon when I saw Terry sitting on the front steps of a mutual friend. I pulled into the drive in front of them, got out, removed my badge case and concealed handgun (I was not in uniform) and placed them on the hood of my truck. Without taking my eyes off Terry, I said, "It's my understanding that you are the one who shoved me from behind after the dance last month. Do we have a problem? If so, come up to my face and tell me."

Terry was at least 2" taller, 20 pounds heavier and 15 years my junior. He had spend his hard time lifting weights and appeared to have strong upper body strength. If he came toward me Plan A was to kick him between the legs and then hit him with a left hook followed by a pirouette and a kick to the knee. If he wasn't down by then, plan B was to grab my stuff and beat it.

Terry, just said, "Ah, you're all right. Come on and have a beer with us."

This incident didn't' do my reputation any harm as the mutual friend spread the word around that I had backed Terry Bartwell down.

Chapter 22
LAST OF THE SQUAD

The young man, in his late teens, pulled into the driveway, eager to show his father and great grandfather his latest acquisition, a '32 Ford. Almost at the same time a delivery man arrived with a package. Taking the carefully wrapped box, with the word "FRAGILE" stamped in red on all sides, into the library of the ancient Tudor style house, he approached a much older man seated in a leather wingback.

"Pop." Then a little louder, "Grandpa, come outside for a minute I want to show you my new car. It's got all the extras."

The old timer knew cars. He had studied, and in some cases rubbed shoulders with, the best of the early engineers, customizers and racers. Men with the immortalized names of Iskenderian, Duntov, Barris, Fangio, Vukovich . . . .

After the ritualistic inspection of the male bonding medium the two men returned to the den where the younger remembered the package. "I almost forgot, Pop, this came for you a little while ago."

"What is it Sonny?" the old man asked, settling into his overstuffed chair.

"I don't know Pop. It's from some police department back east and it sounds like it has liquid in it. You getting your Geritol by mail now?" The great grandson joked.

Staring at the proffered package the old man pushed back further into the cushions of the chair as if trying to distance himself from it. His mouth dropped open . . . "Oh my God", escaped in a barely audible, raspy whisper.

"Grandpa, what's wrong? Are you okay?" The young gentleman crossed the room to take this ancient man's hand and search his frightened stare. "What is it, Pop?"

As recollections of events, forever melded to the sentimental portions of his mind were forced to the present, the great grandfather's eyes soon began refocusing to a new intensity. "Get a couple of glasses and some ice, Sonny - and call your Dad in here. I've got a story to tell you."

A man with graying hair and his teenage son watched the great grandfather, in his 96th year, carefully and ceremoniously unwrap the package. Inside, sealed and encased in a solid wood box with a glass front panel, was a bottle of whisky. Attached to the outside of this shrine was a small brass hammer and a pouch. From this pouch he pulled a sheet of paper containing a list of names - names that had lines drawn through each, save one.

It was a very long time ago that they had met for the last time - a sort of reunion and farewell to one of the members who had but a short time to live.

Pretensions and pressures were checked at the door that night; whatever problems they faced outside seemed far away and not important. Maybe it was seeing a "best" friend for the first time in two or three decades or just that deep feeling that only comes from the knowledge that to this group each truly belonged. They all knew that this assembly was just this night only and never again would they all be together. Maybe it came with the understanding that these were their roots and the distinct sensation of having come home again. Perhaps it was the familiarity and companionship of old friends, whose dues were also paid in full. It was a most memorable occasion.

It was a small and informal gathering, 9 men out of a possible 16 that had all worked together at one time or another in and for the County of Locke. Some had died, some couldn't be found, most were graying and pot bellied, but all had, at one time, stood back-to-back and shoulder-to-shoulder to fight crime and criminals.

"Here, you do it Sonny," the old man said handing the brass hammer to his great grandson. Uncapping the bottle, which had been freed by breaking the glass front and without lifting his eyes from the list, the old man in his articulate way, began to pour forth a tale as if he had been rehearsing it all his life.

"Shooter, that's what they called me because I took my whisky as a straight shot, not because I was the best shot on the department. Using my issue Smith and Wesson Combat Magnum, that included a honed action and custom grips, I fired in the expert level at every practice. All that practice had its price – never enough time for the family and my lovie . . . your grandmother, Jerry," the old man said nodding to the man with graying hair.

"Ah, you boys should have seen my bride! She was just about the prettiest thing that ever rode shotgun in an open convertible. I met her at a hot rod club dance - a sock hop we called it – before I ever became a cop. She wore dungarees with the cuffs rolled up, in giant folds, almost to her knees. Her oversized shirt must have been her daddy's white dress button-down which also had huge folds of the sleeves all the way up her arm. The shirt tails were tied in a knot at her tiny waist, the slightest view of smooth soft skin barely visible. She wore her hair in a pony-tail and she just had that fresh scrubbed look about her. Quite the opposite of me with my axle greased ducktails and form-fitted pink shirt with string tie and pleated slacks of charcoal gray. We rocked and rolled to the likes of Fat's Domino, Dale Wright, Buddy Holly and Larry Williams and when she put her head under my chin to 'Sixteen Candles' I knew it was something special. It was. She accepted my working different shifts, over-time, range practice and all the comes-with stuff of being a police officer with never a complaint. Last week it would have been our 72nd anniversary . . . if she were still alive."

"Grandpa," the impatient teenager interrupted, "What about the bottle?"

"I'm comin' to that, Sonny. Don't rush me. Like I was sayin', it was at this gathering when we all got together for that one last time to say goodbye to Sammy. Sam was sort of like me, an old hot-rodder. Except Sam still had his first rod, a deuce coupe with a 283Chevy engine. He would drive it to practice shoots and an occasional car show.

Now, nothing lasts forever, and by age 50 Sammy had developed a terminal case of cancer. Knowing that he was a short timer he kept himself busy hunting us down and planning this assembly to unite us for one last time and to establish his gift as a tontine - the bottle from which we are drinking at this very moment. He said he won the fifth at an FOP shoot and being a teetotaler, just put it away. Sam, Sammy, was Jewish and for that solemn affair he gave us a little insight into these ancient teachings. It was such a somber and commemorative occasion that I still remember his final words to us. Here was this dying compatriot, frail and weak, who looked each one of us in the eye as he decreed: 'In our faith it is believed that on Rosh Hashana, the New Year, it is written; on Yom Kippur, The Day of Atonement, it is sealed:

> *How many shall pass on,*
> *How many shall come to be,*
> *Who shall live to see ripe age,*
> *And who shall not,*
> *Who shall live,*
> *And who shall die;*

and so it must be, that only the last surviving member of, HAPSS, the Homicide And Police Special Squad of the Locke County Sheriff's Office, may toast his fellow members with – and savor the nectar of this - this last man bottle.'"

"Early in my career there were a number of police killings, assassinations, by anti-government groups such as the Black Panthers and the Weathermen. When our agency lost three, gunned down in cold blood, Sheriff Jackson established a task force to infiltrate these killer gangs. There were sixteen of us, including some federal agents. During this reign of terror and before we were disbanded after Sheriff Jackson was term limited out, we took 35 TOOPs out of circulation. Thirty-one went to prison and five were killed in shoot-outs with HAPSS officers.

"These were horrifying times with confidential informant reports of planned ambushes on cops coming in everyday. Sammy and I, working as partners and fronting a used stereo store, learned that four of our clients – those who were stealing goods to sell to us – were suddenly in the market to buy firearms. The guns were to be used to off cops. Sammy was the kind of guy who had a lot of common sense - the ability to know when to stick your nose in someone else's business and when to ignore him. The business of putting felons away was Sammy's main business.

They trusted us as we had always spoke of our hatred for police. A buy was set up. But when it went down, things didn't work out. Somehow, as I bent to retrieve the ordered weapons, the wire I was wearing was discovered and the head perp, Carmine, drew his nine. Sammy yelled and lunged at the cop killer wannabe as shots began breaking glass and bones. I drew my concealed duty gun and triple tapped Carmine as Sammy rolled to the floor snatching his Colt Detective Special from a Seventrees shoulder rig. He punched holes in two of the other dirtbags while the fourth beat feet out the front door and into the guns of the backup. Sammy had taken a slug to the kidney to save my life."

With a sigh of finality his still steady hand, rough, dried and cracked like a cheap paint job that had crystallized, picked up the small doubles glass. Using both hands, and not unlike how one would make an offering, raised the glass to just slightly above his head whispering, "I'll see you soon fellahs."

Warmed by the energy of the aged whiskey the old man rose from the security of his wingback and shuffled to the leaded windows overlooking the springtime embraced driveway. Just for an instant he was sure he saw Sammy waving from his NINETEEN thirty-two Ford, the one with the hopped-up Chevy engine and the hot rod club plaque dangling from the back bumper. But, a deliberate wipe of the hand across his tear filling eyes revealed it was only his great grandson's . . . brand new TWENTY thirty-two Ford.

****

APPENDIX

AFTERWORD

TRUTHS: Having lived almost seventy years, I have made a few observations and learned a few truths – some the hard way. Many times, while handling a case, reading an inspirational book passage, just watching the TV news report or even in the middle of the night, a though or "truth" would hit me. These musing have, produced over 100 laws not yet on the Books. Also included are several profound statements by others.

Though some seem to be more truthful than others, a select number are smack-your-head, downright undeniable. Such as: The "law" attributed to the Hell's Angels: *"Three can keep a secret . . . if two are dead."* and "Klein's 3rd Law of Survival: *If you're ever in a situation where another person is about to murder you, at that moment, you'd trade all your worldly possessions for a firearm. And, if that threat was to kill your child or your grandchild, you'd sell your soul for a gun."* I have yet to find anyone who can deny these "duh" facts.

AN AMERICAN TRUTH: Law enforcement's role in society is to arrest criminals, not judge them or inflict retribution. Guilt is determined by the court – however:

It is a misconception to believe that if you contest your traffic ticket in court you can convince the judge you are NOT GUILTY. When stopped by the cops for a traffic violation, you are, for all intents and purposes, having your trial right there on the street. When an officer cites you, he is swearing to the facts of your violation. For a judge to determine you are not guilty he would have to find that the officer is lying. Judges won't do that, barring some uncontroverted evidence that this officer was committing misfeasance. Furthermore, a finding of not guilty means you will have a great case to sue the officer, his department and the jurisdiction he represents. Judges don't want that because they're also on the same government dole. Of course, the burden of proof is always on the prosecutor to prove you violated the law - that proof is the officer's sworn testimony - a government agent who is presumed to have no motive to wrongly ticket you. Therefore, and in reality, the burden falls to you to prove he's lying. Now, I know what you're thinking: "I know lots of people who got off . . . ." Getting off due to technicalities or dismissal for other reasons is not the same as a not-guilty finding.

Recently, there has been a push to create a "zero tolerance" for exceeding the speed limits. In all but one or two states the posted speed limits are prima-facie limits - not absolutes. In other words, and in accordance with previous court rulings, unless there are mitigating circumstances, 10 or even more MPH over the limit is not necessarily speeding.

For example, it has been found that if one is going, say 50 MPH in a 40 MPH zone on a clear, dry day with light traffic, it's not speeding. That's why, on all traffic citations, there are spaces to note road, traffic and weather conditions. The exceptions to this rule are school and highway construction zones.

The only time we had absolute speed limits was under the Federal 55 MPH ruling in the late seventies to counter gas shortages. There were two significant problems with absolute limit enforcement: The enforcers found out, one couldn't be cited for driving "too fast for conditions," for example, driving 40 in a 40 zone during a blinding snow storm. The other problem, the public found it was far too Orwellian.

****

176

LAWS NOT ON THE BOOKS:
KLEIN'S LAWS

KLEIN'S 1st LAW:

No Lying, No Cheating, No Stealing. No Exceptions, No Excuses.

COROLLARY TO KLEIN'S FIRST LAW:

Vital Exigent Circumstance integrated with the Lesser of Two Evils Doctrine supersedes all guiding principles.

LAW OF LAWS:

We are NOT a nation of laws - we are a nation of constitutions. Laws, statutes, court decrees, presidential edicts are subservient to constitutions.

CONSTITUTIONAL LAW:

The Constitution should be amended to say: For every new law, statute or ordinance - two must be repealed.

LAW OF AMERICAN JURISPRUDENCE:

American justice may be blindfolded, but human frailties and political pressure tempts peeking by the justices themselves.

LAW OF JUDICIAL IMPARTIALITY:

When a judge imparts his instructions or charges to a jury; that jury is no longer impartial.

LAW OF EMPLOYMENT:

Everyone should have at least one job in his or her lifetime where they start each day with the revelation, 'You mean they pay me to do this?'

LAW OF SALES OR OTHER REQUESTS:
The worst they can do is say No.

177

LAW OF ONE'S DUTY TO SOCIETY:

Everyone should put something back into his or her community.

LAW OF GOVERNMENT:

The number of voters impacted by government-originated funds is directly proportional to the proliferation and power of government and inversely proportional to the ideals of a republic.

LAW OF THE FUTURE:

The longevity of any republic or democracy is dependent upon: The 4th Estate's ability to identify and expose the 5th Column(s) in a manner framed by the 4th Dimension.

THEORY OF TIME:

When it comes to discovering the origins of the universe, all the earth/orbit telescopes, X-ray/radio scopes and infrared/laser gizmos are inconsequential should man conquer the 4th dimension.

COROLLARY TO KLEIN'S THEORY OF TIME:

God may not have provided mere mortals with the ability to conquer the 4th dimension, as thus empowered, man might be tempted to alter His plans and designs.

COROLLARY TO EINSTEIN'S THEORY OF RELATIVITY:

All matters that are not matters of matter, are matters of perspective.

1st LAW OF LIFE:

The secret to life is the ability to adapt to change.

2nd LAW OF LIFE:

To a parent, nothing, absolutely nothing, can emulate the loss of a child.

3rd LAW OF LIFE:

It is a blessing if our parents are spared the pain and anguish of out-living us. We are, however, always astounded to be blessed so soon.

4th LAW OF LIFE:

Living outside the lines tends to spawn euphoric frustrations which ofttimes is the only route to deep personal satisfaction.

5th LAW OF LIFE:

Regrets haunt...not for the things we did, but for the things we didn't do."

6th LAW OF LIFE:

Upon attaining the age of four score, the question that comes to mind is: 'Do I have 20 years, 20 days or 20 minutes?'

7th LAW OF LIFE:

Bad debts, criminal convictions and dishonor may haunt for a lifetime - ask any inmate.

8th LAW OF LIFE:

Good credit, legitimacy and integrity will enhance life - ask anyone who has achieved these attributes.

9th LAW OF LIFE:

Just because we went to high school together, doesn't mean we're friends . . . but if we meet again at our reunion, I'm sure we will be.

1st LAW OF GOD's EXISTENCE:

God exists, because without him we wouldn't.

2nd LAW OF GOD's EXISTENCE:

That inner voice you hear every time you're about to do something wrong. . . is God speaking to you.

3rd LAW OF GOD's EXISTENCE:

God has blessed us all; it's just that some of us have a difficult time recognizing it.

1st LAW OF RIGHTS:

Rights are only such when they don't infringe upon the rights of others. One's right to swing his fist ends where the other person's nose begins. Of course, if one keeps his fist concealed in his pocket he is violating no one's rights. On the same token, for example, if a law-abiding citizen goes about his legal business with a firearm concealed in his pocket he is no more infringing the rights of any other person than the theater-goer who keeps the word "fire" concealed in his mouth.

2nd LAW OF RIGHTS:

All Americans have the right to remain silent; many, however, don't have the ability.

3rd LAW OF RIGHTS:

You have the right to ask me any question you wish, as long as your allow me the right to refuse to answer any question I wish.

4th LAW OF RIGHTS:

There is no statute, law, constitutional right that guarantees that life is fair.

LAW OF SCHOOLS:

Framing the 10 Commandments in our schools might work for some, but posting the first 10 Amendments would work for all.

MARITAL LAW FOR MEN:

Any man who admits to his wife that he can sometimes be dumb, can get away with a lot of dumb stuff.

1st LAW OF COMMON SENSE:

Some people seem to have more dollars than sense.

2nd LAW OF COMMON SENSE:

The middle ground between the far left and ultra right.

3rd LAW OF COMMON SENSE:

The ability to know when to stick your nose in your neighbor's business and when to ignore him.

4th LAW OF COMMON SENSE:

The space between unmitigated hatred and unquestioning faith.

LAW OF THREATS:

It might not be in one's best interest to tell another what to do - without the authority, power and ability to enforce this de facto threat." (see Klein's Laws on Bluffing)

1st LAW OF BLUFFING:

Bluffing one's authority, power or ability is a great tactical move . . . if you pull it off.

2nd LAW OF BLUFFING:

For every bluff tendered, there should be a plan B.

LAW OF DREAMS:

Never being able to satiate aspirations is better than not having any fantasies at all.

LAW OF VOTING:

Any politician that doesn't trust me, a law-abiding, trained citizen, with a firearm to protect myself and my family, clearly cannot be trusted with other matters of importance.

LAW OF OUTRAGE:

The resentment and contempt we gun owners have toward the anti-gunners is not that they are exercising their 1st Amendment right to redress our government - it's the outrage that they work to infringe our 2nd Amendment right via laws and court orders rather than seeking to amend the Constitution.

1st LAW OF SURVIVAL:

The second to last thing a morally responsible, prudent person wants to do is kill another human being regardless of how reprehensible, villainous or dangerous that person might be. The last thing this morally responsible, prudent person wants to do is be killed by that reprehensible, villainous and dangerous person.

2nd LAW OF SURVIVAL:

All the rules, statutes, restraining orders, 911 calls, hand to hand combat techniques, aerosol spray Mace or other pseudo protective measures will never equal the effectiveness of a firearm when faced with an unwarranted and deadly criminal attack.

3rd LAW OF SURVIVAL:

If you're ever in a situation where another person is about to murder you, at that moment, you'd trade all your worldly possessions for a firearm. And, if that threat was to kill your child or your grandchild, you'd sell your soul for a gun.

4th LAW OF SURVIVAL:

Knowing how to shoot is the easy part. Knowing when is the important part.

5th LAW OF SURVIVAL:

Losing a gun battle is forever; but the aftermath of surviving a firefight, with the possibility of criminal prosecution and civil suit, might be worse.

6th LAW OF SURVIVAL:

If you believe that psychological tough talk will enable you to bluff your way out of a dangerous situation, you might be wrong...dead wrong. Super-predators - losers with nothing to lose - can't be bluffed.

7th LAW OF SURVIVAL:

There's lots worse things than being killed by some thug - one is: watching a family member die at the hands of this thug because you were to much of a fool - or coward - to carry a gun.

8th LAW OF SURVIVAL:

If all the guns in the world could somehow be magically removed; the weak, frail and vulnerable would have no way of protecting themselves from the thugs with bats, clubs and knives.

9th LAW OF SURVIVAL:

All Americans have the inherent and constitutional right to be free of fear from armed citizens. However, this right does not extend to usurping or disparaging other American's inalienable 2nd and 9th Amendment rights to be free of fear from thugs intent on doing them harm.

10th LAW OF SURVIVAL:

Proper training is the key to surviving attacks - lethal as well as litigious.

11th LAW OF SURVIVAL:

Always fight a fair fight - by your definition of fair, of course.

12th LAW OF SURVIVAL:

Always error on the side of force.

13th LAW OF SURVIVAL:

A two-pronged premeditated attack is better than a defensive retaliation.

14th LAW OF SURVIVAL:

In the opening round of any battle, never strike less than twice.

15th LAW OF SURVIVAL:

Self preservation notwithstanding, toe to heal battles are for heals.

16th LAW OF SURVIVAL:

Survival depends upon paranoia becoming prudence long before pogroms and flying bullets.

LAW OF GENEROSITY:

The measure of one's generosity is not how much, but how much in relation to how much is available.

DEFINITION OF POLITICAL CORRECTNESS:

A rhetorician, with a virtuosity complex, who ignores the rule of law to further a political agenda.

LAW OF PSEUDO RACIAL DISCRIMINATION:

It does not make one a racist if they don't want to live next to or go to school with or frequent a business where certain persons flaunt an attitude, dress in prison garb, use foul language, trash the neighborhood, commit crimes or force their music on them . . . none of which have anything to do with race, religion or national origin.

LAW OF AMERICANIZATION:

Those who fail to assimilate, to meld into the melting pot, are doomed to being the outcast.

LAW OF QUID PRO QUO:

In a Republic, if the Government takes your property under their powers of eminent domain, they must compensate you. They also have the power to lay taxes to build and maintain roads, sewers and other needs that benefit the entire community. But there is no quid pro quo when your tax money is given to victims of hurricanes, floods or other natural - but insurable - catastrophes.

LAW OF WAITING:

The length of the wait in any waiting room is inversely proportional to the quality of the reading material.

LAW OF JAIL CROWDING:

The number of police officers in any political jurisdiction is directly proportional to the number of persons arrested and inversely proportional to the time of incarceration.

LAW OF THEFT:

Never steal less than you can successfully hide and comfortably retire on - after you get out of prison.

LAW OF IRONY:

A liberal is one who will staunchly support to the death all of his fellow American's constitutional rights - except one, the 2nd Amendment. Ironically that's the one he might need to successfully win the fight.

LAW OF COPS & ROBBERS:

It's just as exciting to be the chaser as it is the chasee; the significant difference being, the chaser gets to go home at night and then do it again the next day.

1st LAW OF PUBLIC SAFETY:

Any firefighter or police officer who doesn't believe that cowardice is a fate worse than death, is in the wrong business.

2nd LAW OF PUBLIC SAFETY:

The American Police Officer: A balance of benevolence to the community with enforcement of the law, in concert to the Constitution, all the while adhering to highest moral and ethical ideals.

LAW OF SOCIETAL PERPETUATION:

The survival of any society is dependent upon the balance of pro-active to re-active enforcement of its laws.

1st LAW OF CRIMINAL ACTIVITY:

Carry on fool, Hell ain't half full.

2nd LAW OF CRIMINAL ACTIVITY:

The amount of time spent engaging in illegal conduct is directly proportional to chances of incarceration and inversely proportional to honoring family, country and self.

LAW OF WORDS:

Never argue semantics with a writer - it's their stock in trade.

1st LAW OF PLANET EARTH:

We all live up/down wind/stream from each other.

2nd LAW OF PLANET EARTH:

Thou shalt not harvest or sell any wild animal or plant for commercial purposes.

3rd LAW OF PLANET EARTH: When international demand exceeds supply of finite resources, war is inevitable.

4th LAW OF PLANET EARTH:

Unless we voluntarily return to pre-1900 world population levels - global warming/cooling, pollution and/or famine - will do it for us.

5th LAW OF PLANET EARTH:

The infiniteness of world population is inversely proportional to the finiteness of natural resources.

LAW OF DISASTER SURVIVAL:

Disaster Survival is more a state of mind than the amount of supplies you can put away.

1st LAW OF LEGACY:

Though some might last longer and/or have greater impact - all are subjective as everyone leaves a legacy.

2nd LAW OF LEGACY:

Moral man has only two goals in life - To honor the integrity of his ancestors and to sow these seeds for his descendants.

1st LAW OF CONFLICT RESOLUTION:

The one who wins the most battles is the one who chooses which battles to enter.

2nd LAW OF CONFLICT RESOLUTION:

Sometimes it's advantageous to purposely lose a battle in order to win the war.

LAW OF HAPPINESS:

Happiness is being guilt free.

1st LAW OF HISTORY:

History, in and of itself, is just memories. Memories, coupled with extrapolation, are the lessons of history.

2nd LAW OF HISTORY:

Christians and Jews are the epitome of decent, law-abiding, productive citizens; and as such, have raised the moral, ethical and living standards of all peoples.

LAW OF MEMORIES:

The best memories are those that are forever melded to the sentimental portion of the mind.

LAW OF VISION:

Some have trouble seeing the forest for the trees while others seem to be troubled seeing the trees for the forest.

LAW OF CREATING IDEAS:

Play solitaire. Sleep on it. Repeat as necessary

LAW OF CREATIVITY:

Little people talk about people; regular people talk about things; creative people talk about ideas.

1st LAW OF WISDOM:

Youth is fraught with the futility of convincing your parents you know what you're doing. Parenthood is fraught with the futility of imparting your wisdom upon your children. Grand parenting is fraught with futility of observing your children trying to impart wisdom on your grandchildren.

2nd LAW OF WISDOM:

One's level of wisdom is measured more by the ability to learn from the successes and failures of others, than by one's own triumphs and mistakes.

LAW OF GRANDPARENTING:

Grand parenting generates a capacity to love far greater than you ever thought possible.

1st LAW OF CHRISTMAS:

Christmas is an American National Holiday. It ALSO might be a religious holy day, or a holiday in other countries, but it is - in the United States of America - a de facto, official, certified, recognized National Holiday. Ramadan, Chanukah, etc. are not.

2nd LAW OF CHRISTMAS:

The Christmas Tree may or may not be a religious symbol, but it most assuredly is a representation of Santa Claus and our National Holiday. As such, it belongs on government property.

3rd LAW OF CHRISTMAS:

Placing a decorated Christmas tree, sans religious ornamentation, in the public domain is expected, proper and an American tradition. Manger scenes, Menorahs or KKK crosses are a different matter and have no standing for placement on public property.

1st LAW OF CHRISTMAS GREETINGS:

To wish someone a Merry Christmas, doesn't necessarily mean that you wish them anything other than they have a happy 25th of December. Nor does it mean that you, if not a Christian, are accepting their beliefs or forsaking yours.

2nd LAW OF CHRISTMAS GREETINGS:

For a Christian to wish a non-Christian a merry Christmas is the epitome of what this special day is all about. The Christian is saying, "This is my special day and I wish that your day will be as wonderful as my day promises to be."

3rd LAW OF CHRISTMAS GREETINGS:

For a non-Christian to receive "Merry Christmas" from a Christian is a great compliment as in, here a fellow

American God-fearing, decent, Judeo-Christian-valued person is wishing me a good day. "Thank you."

4th LAW OF CHRISTMAS GREETINGS:

When a non-Christian wishes a Christian a merry Christmas, he or she is saying, "I applaud and honor your right to celebrate this day that stands for the good in mankind and our common values that make this country what it is . . . and thanks for the day off.

1st LAW OF CHRISTMAS WISHES:

To my fellow non-Christian friends: Please join me in honoring this day by reflecting on how fortunate we are to live in a country that not only allows us to choose and practice our own religion, but protects these rights.

2nd LAW OF CHRISTMAS WISHES:

To religious fundamentalists, be they Christian, Jewish, atheist, Muslim, etc.: Please recognize that when you try to force your beliefs on others with guns, law suits, government sanctification or "majority rule" you're not exhibiting American values, merely, your own insecurities.

3rd LAW OF CHRISTMAS WISHES:

To the little kids (of all religions) who are able to grasp Santa Claus and really don't understand religious matter: Enjoy. It's the only time in your life you will be happily conned and guilt free.

****

OTHER'S TRUTHS & LAWS NOT ON THE BOOKS

HENRY WILLIAMSON'S LAW OF RIGHTS:

A right is not a right if it takes someone else to make it happen.

Lt. UMBAUGH'S LAW:

One either never carries a firearm, or one always carries, but one never sometimes carries.

TOM HYMAN'S LAW OF FRIENDSHIP:

Friendship trumps moments of emotional stupidity and forgiveness trumps pride.

LAW OF TROUBLE:

Temper is what gets most of us into trouble; Pride is what keeps us there.

FOOLS LAW:

It is better to remain silent and be thought a fool, than to open your mouth and remove all doubt.

LOVIE'S LAW:

I'm not whining, I'm just reiterating the facts.

GEORGE W. BUSH'S LAW OF JUSTICE:

Whether we bring our enemies to justice or bring justice to our enemies, justice will be done.

CHUCK'S LAW OF BUSINESS:

Little troubles now, big troubles later.

BREADWINNERS LAW:

Most breadwinners lead lives of quiet desperation.

HELL'S ANGELS LAW:

Three can keep a secret . . . if two are dead.

LAW OF POLITICAL PARTIES:

The Conservative is the one who was robbed last night; The Liberal is the one who was arrested last night; The Libertarian is the one who shot the robber last night.

LAW OF STATURE:

Better to be an old has-been than a never has-been.

LAW OF EXPERIENCE:

One who claims to have ten years experience might only have one year's experience ten times.

SIR EDWARD GREY'S LAW OF THE UNITED STATES:

A gigantic boiler. Once the fire is lighted under it there is no limit to the power it can generate.

BORDER PATROLMAN BILL JORDAN'S LAW OF GUNFIGHTS:

There are no second place winners.

LAW OF WINNING:

The next best thing to playing and winning, is playing and losing.

LAW OF MARRIAGE:

Everyone experiences three loves; The one they marry, the one they're glad they didn't marry and the one that got away.

OLD JEWISH LAW OF LIFE:

You get too pushy. . . nobody likes you.

OLD COUNTRY LAW:

The door might not always be locked, but the gun is always loaded.

LAW OF MOTOR VEHICLE OPERATION:

Keep the rubber side down.

MOTORCYCLE RIDER'S LAW:

There are old motorcycle riders and there are bold motorcycle riders, but there are no old, bold motorcycle riders.

POLICE OFFICERS LAW OF I.D.:

Badges? We don't got to show you no stinkin' badges.

POLITICIANS LAW OF THE GOLDEN RULE:

What's mine is mine and what's yours is mine.

RICH MAN'S LAW OF THE GOLDEN RULE:

He who has the gold, makes the rules.

DESPOT'S LAW OF THE GOLDEN RULE:

Do unto others before they do unto to you.

WW2 FACTORY LAW (Also good for Bachelor Parties, etc.):

What you see here, what you hear here, let it stay here when you leave here.

EDUCATION vs. EXPERIENCE LAW:

Education is what you get from reading the small print; experience is what you get from not reading it.

****

GLOSSARY/
COMMON POLICE AND FIREARM TERMS

Police officers may be experts at firearms use-of-force, but far too many have misunderstandings of the terms used when report-writing about guns. This lack of knowledge is not limited to cops as one noted author penned, ". . . he grabbed the 30.06 rifle . . . ." The thirty-ought-six is probably the most well-known cartridge in the world. However, it is displayed as .30-06. The ".30" is the caliber or bore diameter of the barrel (in hundredths of an inch). The "06" refers to the year (1906) when the cartridge was accepted by and for the U.S. Military. Another noted author, when describing a group of men in a story set in the early 1970s, had one of them shooting a Glock pistol. Glock didn't make handguns until the 1980s.

Other egregious errors found in news media stories, articles, books and police reports include:

"The gun used was a Colt automatic" (Did the writer mean machinegun or the more common SEMI-automatic? Colt has made both).

"He took out his pistol, opened the cylinder...." (Pistols don't have cylinders – only revolvers do).

"The killer placed a fresh bullet into his gun" (I think he means, Cartridge).

ACP: Automatic Colt Pistol. The most common guns/cartridges run from the diminutive .25 ACP to the heavy on the stopping power .45 ACP.

AKA/a.k.a./aka: Also Known As.

BALLISTICS: Science of the characteristics of projectiles in motion. *Interior ballistics* cover the time between the start of primer ignition and the bullet's exit from the barrel. *Exterior ballistics* encompass the bullet's flight from the barrel exit to the point of impact with a target. *Terminal ballistics* is the study of occurrences after the projectile impacts the target.

BARREL: Part of the firearm through which the discharged bullet passes moving from breach to muzzle.

BORE: The inside of the barrel through which the discharged bullet passes. Size is determined by measuring the distance between the lands or groves of a rifled barrel or maximum inside diameter of a smoothbore (shotgun) barrel.

BULLET: (aka PROJECTILE) The missile only. The part of the cartridge that separates, exits from the muzzle and impacts on the target.

CALIBER: Refers to a weapon's (land or grove) or bullet's diametrical size - usually expressed in hundredths of an inch or metric equivalent. Sometimes includes other information to indicate powder charge (e.g., .38-40) or year of adoption (e.g., .30-06) or special designation (e.g., .38 Special).

CARTRIDGE: A complete unit of ammunition which is comprised of the cartridge case, primer, propellant, and bullet - a loaded round of ammunition.

CHAMBER: Inside portion of the breech formed to accommodate the cartridge.

CLIP: Device to hold cartridges for insertion into a cylinder or magazine. See "MAGAZINE".

CODES, RADIO:

Code 2: Respond at once without emergency lights and siren.

Code 3: Respond at once using emergency lights and siren.

Code 4: No further assistance required. Disregard previous transmission.

Code 7: Out of service (2-7) for a meal break.

CYLINDER: Revolving mechanical part of a revolver which houses multiple chambers.

DOA/D.O.A.: Dead on Arrival. A person who is (or will be declared) dead upon arrival at the hospital. The term is also used to describe anything that is defunct such as, "Your proposal/idea/game is DOA."

FIREARM: Any weapon from which a projectile(s) is discharged by means of a rapidly burning or exploding propellant.

FRAME: The non-moveable mechanical portion of a weapon that all other parts are attached and to which the serial number is imprinted.

FTO: Field Training Officer. A police officer who conducts training while on-duty and on patrol.

GRIP: See "STOCK"

GSW: Gun Shot Wound

HAMMER: Moveable mechanical part of the action which, when released, drives the firing pin into the primer.

HANDGUN: A firearm (revolver or pistol) designed to be operated with one hand and without the aid of extraneous support.

HOMICIDE: The killing of a human being, accidental or purposely.

INSTINCT COMBAT SHOOTING: The act of operating a HANDGUN by focusing on the target and instinctively coordinating the hand and mind to cause the handgun to discharge at a time and point that ensures interception of the target with the projectile. Method developed by and term coined by Police Firearms Instructor CHUCK KLEIN. His book by the same name has been in continuous print for over 25 years and taught in police academies worldwide.

INSTINCT SHOOTING: (aka point shooting) Focusing on the target and instinctively shooting any long gun without the aid or use of mechanical sights.

LE or LEO: Law Enforcement or Law Enforcement Officer.

MAGAZINE: Removable part of a pistol which holds cartridges in such a way as to facilitate the chambering of these cartridges during operational functioning.

MALFEASANCE: The unjust performance of an act which a person has no right to do.

MISFEASANCE: The doing of a lawful act in an unlawful manner.

MO: Method of Operation. How one conducts business.

MURDER: The willful killing of a human being by another.

MUZZLE: The end of the barrel from which the discharged projectile exits.

NCIC: National Crime Information Center. Computer system housing information on wanted persons and vehicles, plus stolen items with serial numbers (firearms). Early contact was via teletype. In the field, LEOs would request a query, such as QW or QV (see QUERIES) by radio. The dispatch center would then type in the information on a teletype and send it to NCIC in Washington, D.C. Results could be as quick as a minute or up to hours depending upon demand and status of the computers.

NON-FEASANCE: The failure to perform an act one is required to do.

OIC: Officer in Charge

PERP: Police slang for perpetrator (criminal).

PISTOL: aka: Autoloader, auto pistol, semi-auto. Any self-loading handgun that is not a revolver. Usually incorporates the chamber as part of the barrel. Requires the manually pulling and releasing of the trigger for each shot. After each shot the recoil "automatically" pushes the slide rearward, ejecting the spent cartridge, cocking the hammer/firing pin and, on the return forward movement, striping a fresh cartridge from the magazine for insertion into the chamber. This action/reaction does not disengage the sear, which can only be done by releasing the trigger.

Fully automatic weapons such as machine guns or submachine guns will continue to fire until either the trigger is released or the magazine is emptied.

POINT BLANK RANGE: Distance so close that appreciable projectile deviation of line of flight is negligible.

PRIMA FACIE: On its face. At first sight. A fact presumed to be true until disproved.

****

198

QUERIES:

QW: Short for Query Wanted. It's used as a request of the dispatcher to run a file check to learn if a certain person is wanted on warrants or is known to be dangerous.

QV: Short for Query Vehicle. This is used to request the dispatcher to make a file check to learn if a vehicle's license plate number or VIN is on the wanted or stolen list.

QCH: Short for Query Criminal History. Used to check the police computer system for the arrest record of a person. It can be accessed by name plus DOB or by SSN.

REVOLVER: A multi-shot handgun, utilizing a revolving cylinder as a cartridge receptacle.

SAFETY: Any device or mechanism which locks or blocks the trigger, hammer and/or sear to prevent unintentional discharge.

SEMI-AUTOMATIC: See "PISTOL"

SHOTGUN: A shoulder fired long-gun with a smooth (not rifled) barrel. Shotguns can shoot slugs (single massive bullets), or shot-shells (cartridges) loaded with shot (multiple round pellets) Shot size runs from smaller than BBs to much larger than BBs.

SIGNALS, RADIO: Though not uniform by any measure, some signals and codes were universally accepted during the time period of these stories.

Signal 2: Spoken as Signal-two. In most jurisdictions it means to respond to the station.

Signal 20: Spoken as Signal-twenty, meaning injured person.

Signal 26: Spoken as two-six meaning in-service as in an officer is on-duty and available for details/assignments.

Signal 27: Spoken as two-seven. Officially it means out-of-service as in the officer is going off the air to handle a detail. In days before individual officer radios, every time an officer was out of his cruiser (away from the car mounted radio) he advised the dispatcher he was 2-7. Two-Seven also could unofficially denote a deceased person (the perp is 2-7) or a fellow officer who is "not with it" or asleep (shh, the Lieutenant is 2-7).

Signal 30: Spoken as Signal-thirty. Wanted person, vehicle or firearm. An officer receiving such a radio transmission is being told the person with him (or vehicle/firearm queried) is a wanted or dangerous person .

SIGNAL 44: Spoken as Signal-forty-four or car number followed by 44, meaning, what is your location (Four-six-eight, forty-four)?

Signal: 10-4: Spoken as Ten-four. Okay. I acknowledge your transmission.

Signal: 10-78: Spoken as Ten-seventy-eight. Officer needs help.

SNUB-NOSE: Slang term usually meaning any short barreled revolver.

SO. Sheriff's office or Sheriff's department

STOCK: Portion of the weapon which is held in or by the hand.

SWAT: Special Weapons And Tactics. A team of specially trained and equipped LEOs who can muster and respond quickly when lethal force conditions require.

TACHYINTERVAL: Time-deception phenomena. A condition that occurs when, under extreme stress, events appear to happen in slow motion. Events, of course, do not slow down but, the mind seems to speed up due to the

200

brains ability to digest information much faster than the body can act/react. Many people who have been in serious auto accidents or gun fights have experienced this condition.

TOOP: Police slang for perps, dirtbags - persons who are: Temporarily Out Of Prison.

TRAJECTORY: The parabolic path of a projectile in flight from muzzle to impact.

TRIGGER: Moveable mechanical device designed to be operated by the index finger for double action or single action mode depending on type of firearm.

TUNNEL-VISION: Peripheral-optic distortion/dysfunction phenomena. A condition that can occur during high concentration where one sees (is aware of) only the center of his/hers attention. This temporary occurrence renders the victim oblivious to surrounding events.

VIN: Vehicle Identification Number. An automobile's serial number.

SOME COMMON HANDGUN CALIBERS:

.22 Long Rifle (.22LR) This is a rim fire cartridge and has been very popular for over 100 years.

.25 ACP. Small cartridge for small handguns.

.380 Automatic. Popular self-defense pistol round.

9mm Lugar. Once popular police cartridge.

.38 Special. Early police revolver cartridge – still popular in snub-nose revolvers.

.357 Magnum. Popular revolver cartridge for police and self-protection.

.40 Caliber. Popular modern police pistol cartridge.

.44 Magnum. Powerful hunting and self-defense handgun round.

.45 ACP Thought developed prior to 1911, it is still a popular police and self-defense pistol round.

BIOGRAPHICAL INFORMATION
Chuck Klein

 In addition to duties as a full-time certified police officer for Woodlawn and Terrace Park, Ohio, Klein also served with the Switzerland County, Indiana Sheriff's office, was police photography instructor for the Norwood, Ohio Police Academy and a staff instructor for Tactical Defense Institute (www.tdiohio.com) . Though not an attorney, he holds a Bachelor of Laws degree from Blackstone School of Law and is an active member of the International Association of Law Enforcement Firearms Instructors (IALEFI). Contact and additional information may be found on his web site: www.chuckklein.com

Also by Chuck Klein:

GUNS IN THE WORKPLACE, A Manual for Private Sector Employers and Employees

INSTINCT COMBAT SHOOTING, Defensive Handgunning for Police

CIRCA 1957

LINES OF DEFENSE, Police Ideology and the Constitution

KLEIN'S CCW HANDBOOK, The Requisite for Those Who Carry Concealed Weapons

KLEIN'S UNIFORM FIREARMS POLICY, A manual for Private Sector Detectives and Security Agents

THE POWER OF GOD

LAWS & IDEAS, Truths and Observations, Plus a Formula for Originating Ideas

From BeachHouse-Hot Rods and Romance

The Way It Was-- Nostalgic Tales of Hotrods and Romance Chuck Klein (2003) Series of hotrod stories by author of Circa 1957 in collaboration with noted illustrator Bill Lutz BeachHouse Books edition 5½ X 8½, 200 pp ISBN: 1-888725-86-9

The Way It Was
Nostalgic Tales of HotRods and Romance

Chuck Klein

"...a delightful mix of anecdote, observation, and social history. A book so masterfully written, you can almost smell new upholstery on the street rod. This is definitely the best read..."

Paul Taylor, Publisher. Route 66 Magazine

"...a classic recipe for hours of delightful entertainment.... If this is your first time reading Chuck Klein, it's just like eating chocolate. Once you have the first bite, you know you'll be coming back for more. "

Carl Cartisano, Cruisin' Style Magazine

a new American classic, conjuring up images of good, clean fun for the "hot-rodders" of yesterday and today....a fun, fast read that appeals to the kid in all of us." --

Aaron Lasky, Hot Rod DeLuxe, CK DeLuxe, & Kingpin Magazines

"Your book is great. You have captured the feel and texture of the 'fifties in each story. It's a wonderful read ...which accurately portrays and preserves the magic of the era".

Dusty Rhodes, WSAI Radio, Cincinnati

"Bet you can't read just one!"

Michael Lund, Author of the Growing Up on Route 66 Series

204

8616994R0

Made in the USA
Charleston, SC
27 June 2011